MURDER ON THE THAMES

An Augusta Peel Mystery Book 6

EMILY ORGAN

The Augusta Peel Series

Death in Soho
Murder in the Air
The Bloomsbury Murder
The Tower Bridge Murder
Death in Westminster
Murder on the Thames
The Baker Street Murders

Chapter 1

SHE DIDN'T SUSPECT the man was following her until she turned into Crossfield Lane. He remained twenty yards behind her, just as he had for the past ten minutes. She didn't like his lithe, loping gait or the way he kept his head bowed.

She stopped and turned, hoping the sign she had noticed would ward him off. He lit a cigarette, then loped on past her, his gaze fixed firmly on the ground. He was young and lean and had a scar on his cheek. She gave a shudder as he passed. Something didn't feel right.

She watched him walk on and turn left at the end of the road into Deptford High Street.

She went on her way, enjoying the evening spring sunshine. The days were getting longer now, and the weather was warming up. She forgot about the scar-faced man and thought about the forthcoming May Day celebrations. One of her friends had been chosen as the May Queen and she was looking forward to watching the parade on Deptford Broadway.

She turned right into the high street and stopped at the

sweet shop to buy a bag of pear drops. Then she continued on her way home. As she entered Watergate Street, her nerves returned. It was much quieter than the high street. Was it possible the scar-faced man would reappear? She told herself she was being foolish, but quickened her step.

A man stepped out of a doorway in front of her. She almost collided with him. She was about to comment that he should have looked where he was going, but thought better of it. He was tall and broad, and his eyes were dark. Unnerved, she side-stepped him. But as she walked on, she saw the scar-faced man step out of Queen's Street.

He had continued following her. He must have run around the block and turned back on himself.

She spun round, but she was caught between both men now. Her heart thudded heavily, and her mouth felt dry.

Her only hope was the little alleyway which linked up with Armada Street. She took in a breath, then made a bolt for it.

The cobbles were uneven and it was difficult to run fast. She could hear the footsteps of the men behind her. She threw the bag of pear drops on the ground, vainly hoping they could create a small obstacle.

She ran faster than she had ever run before. Her throat grew sore as she gasped in air.

Cold prickles ran up and down her spine. She *had* to get away.

The alleyway turned to the right and pain shot through her right ankle as she twisted her foot on the cobblestones. Up ahead, she could see Armada Street. Surely someone there could help? A lady with a pram passed by at the end of the alleyway. She was little more than a silhouette, but perhaps it was possible to cry out to her.

She gave a shout as a hand grasped her shoulder. She was moving too fast to put up any resistance. A strong

2

shove sent her tumbling to the ground. She flung her arms around her head. She had to do what she could to protect herself.

But as the second man caught up with her, she knew she was powerless.

Chapter 2

'TODAY IS THE DAY,' said Philip. 'I'm officially open for business. What do you think, Augusta?' He stood in the centre of the bare, high-ceilinged room, leaning on his walking stick. A filing cabinet occupied one corner of the room, and a desk and two chairs were positioned by the window. A notebook and pen were laid neatly on the desk.

'It looks... simple.'

'Simple?'

'Yes. But I suppose this is how everything looks when you start at the very beginning, doesn't it?' Philip had recently left his job as a Detective Inspector at Scotland Yard and was starting his new business as a private detective. He was renting the rooms above Augusta's bookshop in Bloomsbury for his office. 'It feels like there's something missing,' she added.

'What can possibly be missing? I've got a desk, a couple of chairs, and a filing cabinet.'

'Yes, you have the essentials here. It's just a little spartan.'

He nodded. 'I can see why you say that. But I don't like

4

a lot of fussy objects in a room. They get in the way and collect dust.'

'You don't need much. Maybe some pictures on the wall.'

'Pictures of what?'

'I don't know. Perhaps you could visit a gallery and buy some you like.'

'I've just left my job. I don't have a salary at the moment, and I certainly don't have money to spend on art.'

'I don't mean anything expensive. There'll be a shop nearby where you can buy some second-hand pictures.'

'I'd prefer to let you choose them for me, Augusta. I don't know much about art.'

Augusta walked over to the filing cabinet and opened its drawers. Each one was empty. She tried to hide a smile but failed.

'What's so funny?' asked Philip.

'The empty drawers.'

'What do you expect? I don't have any clients yet. I'm hoping the filing cabinet will soon be full.'

'It will be. Oh, I'm sorry for laughing, Philip. I don't know why I find this amusing. I admire you for leaving your job to set up on your own. It can be difficult to begin with.'

'It can. But I've placed advertisements in the main newspapers and I'm hoping that I'll soon receive a call or a visit from a client.'

'And just think of what the future holds. In six months' time, this could be a busy office,' said Augusta. 'You might even need to employ a secretary.'

Philip walked over to his desk, opened a drawer, and took out a small card which he handed to Augusta. It read, "Mr P. N. Fisher, Private Detective" and printed underneath was the office address and a familiar telephone number.

'I can't afford to have a telephone put in just yet, Augusta, so I thought I could borrow yours. If that's alright? I'll contribute towards the monthly bill.'

'Of course. Fred and I can answer it and pretend to be your secretaries.'

'No, I don't want you doing that. I'll dash down the stairs when I hear the telephone ringing.'

Augusta glanced at his walking stick. 'Dash?'

'I can move at a fair speed if I need to.'

A knock at the door interrupted them.

'Perhaps that's your first customer?' said Augusta.

Philip answered the door. 'Oh, it's you, Fred.'

Fred stepped into the room. 'It looks like you're all ready for business, Philip.'

'Yes, I am. And for a moment we thought you were my first customer.'

'Oh, I'm sorry to get your hopes up. I actually need to ask Augusta's permission regarding a dog.'

'Which dog?' said Augusta.

'My friend, Boris, has just called in and he would like to know if he can bring his dog into the shop. It's pouring with rain out there.' Fred nodded towards the window where rain was lashing against the pane. 'He's only a little dog.'

'Of course!' said Augusta. 'We don't want the poor little thing getting soaked out there.'

Chapter 3

'HE MAKES a lot of noise for a little dog,' said Philip a few moments later. A constant yapping bark rose from the shop beneath them.

'Perhaps it was a mistake to allow him in,' said Augusta. 'I'll go and see what's going on.'

She left Philip's office and headed for the door which opened out onto the mezzanine level of her shop. As soon as she opened it, a bundle of wet, frizzy fur launched itself at her legs and snagged her stockings with its claws.

'Titus!' A young, gangly man with a moustache was running up the stairs, two at a time. Augusta guessed he was Fred's friend, Boris. 'Oh goodness, I'm so sorry, madam.' He stooped to pick up the dog who ducked out of his way and cantered back down the stairs, barking excitedly.

'Titus!' Boris followed him and Augusta examined the hole in her stockings. It was annoying, but she kept a spare pair in her handbag. She made her way down the stairs as Titus ran in circles around the shop.

'Can you put him on a lead?' she called out, trying to make herself heard above the dog's barking.

'We're trying!' said Fred. Titus was too quick for the pair of them, and he clearly viewed the chase as a fun game.

'I've got him!' said Augusta as the little animal ran towards her up the stairs. She bent down to get hold of him, but he jumped over her hands and continued on up the stairs back to the mezzanine level. His athleticism was impressive. She couldn't understand why Boris had let him off the lead.

Augusta walked down to the shop floor, and Titus soon joined her. The chase continued with the dog clearly enjoying every moment. Boris lolloped after him, his limbs flailing helplessly. Now and again he scolded the small dog, but it made no difference. His lack of authority over the animal was frustrating. Fred got hold of Titus, but quickly released his grip when the dog snapped at his hand. Sparky the canary watched the spectacle from the safety of his cage on the counter, his head cocked with interest.

A lady stepped into the shop, appeared to think better of it, then left again.

'Great!' said Augusta. 'We've lost a customer!'

'I'm so sorry,' mumbled Boris. 'He's such a naughty dog.'

As Titus ran up to the mezzanine level again, Augusta could feel her patience wearing thin. 'What we need is a big net to catch him in,' she said. 'Where could we get one?'

Fred shrugged. He was out of breath from running around the shop. 'A fisherman?'

Augusta sighed and glanced at her telephone. 'Perhaps we could telephone the dog warden.'

'I'm sure there's no need,' said Fred. 'Boris will catch him before long.'

'And how many customers will we lose in the meantime?'

She noticed Boris sitting on the stairs, trying to catch his breath. She wanted to admonish him for his poor dog-owning skills, but the young man's expression was already bleak. She reasoned he was learning the hard way.

The dog had stopped barking, and she heard movement at the top of the stairs. Looking up, she saw Philip with the dog under his arm as he carefully manoeuvred himself down the stairs with his walking stick.

'Does this little chap belong to you?' he asked Boris.

'Yes, he does. You caught him! Thank you so much.' He held his arms out for the dog.

'We need to get a lead on him before I hand him back to you,' said Philip. 'I don't want to hear that racket all over again.'

Boris apologised repeatedly as Philip descended the stairs. Then Boris took the lead from his jacket pocket and attached it to Titus's collar while Philip was still holding him. Philip carefully placed the little dog on the floor.

'There we go,' he said. 'All is calm.'

'How did you do it?' asked Augusta.

'I think he'd worn himself out by the time I got to him,' said Philip. 'And I'm used to dealing with my mischievous dachshund, Herbert. I swear that smaller dogs are three times the trouble of larger ones.'

After more apologising, Boris was keen to leave the shop.

'I don't think he'll be back in a hurry,' said Fred.

'Good,' said Philip. 'I've got nothing against him personally, but he should learn how to be a responsible dog owner.' There was a pause as Augusta and Fred nodded in agreement. 'I often wonder how Herbert is faring,' Philip continued. 'I miss that little dog. He's living with my wife and son on the south coast now.'

Philip rarely mentioned his estranged wife, and Augusta wondered if he had seen his young son recently.

'Anyway.' He turned to the window as he changed the subject. 'Look at all that rain out there. It's not very seasonable for the first day of May. I hope it improves for tomorrow. Haven't you got a boat trip planned, Augusta?'

She gave a groan as she recalled it. 'Yes, I have. A boat trip with Cousin Jennifer. Hopefully it will be rained off.'

Chapter 4

THE FOLLOWING day dawned warm and bright, and Augusta's boat trip departed Westminster Pier promptly at ten o'clock.

'How exciting!' said Cousin Jennifer. 'I've never been on a boat trip on the Thames before!'

Jennifer had girlish mannerisms, even though she was no younger than thirty-five. Her protruding front teeth caused her to speak with a lisp, and she had a little upturned nose. Augusta knew her as Cousin Jennifer, but she was a second cousin who she recalled meeting once when she was about ten years old. A distant aunt had written to Augusta a month previously, informing her that Cousin Jennifer was visiting London and Augusta's company for a day would be appreciated. Augusta had reluctantly agreed, and Fred was looking after the shop in her absence.

'Where is this boat going?' asked Jennifer.

'Richmond-upon-Thames,' said Augusta. 'Don't you recall me telling you that?'

'Did you? I must have forgotten. Richmond-upon-Thames sounds very pretty. Is it?'

'I suppose it is.'

'How lovely.'

They sat on a long wooden bench on the starboard side of the boat. They had twisted themselves sideways to look out across the river. The sun's rays were dazzling on the water, and a cool, brisk breeze flapped the canvas awning above their heads.

'That's the Houses of Parliament, isn't it?' said Jennifer. 'How old is it?'

'The building or parliament itself?'

'Isn't it the same thing?'

'Not really.'

'Why not?'

Augusta felt too weary to explain much detail about either. 'Look, we're coming up to a bridge,' she said to distract Jennifer.

'That's a pretty bridge.'

'Lambeth Bridge.'

'How lovely. And I can see some trees over there. There are lots of trees in London, aren't there?'

'Yes, quite a few.'

'Mother told me you own a bookshop.'

'Yes, it's a second-hand bookshop. You're more than welcome to visit.'

'You're very kind, but I'm afraid I don't read books. I don't get on with them very well.'

'Why not?'

'I'm not very good at sitting down and reading. I find myself so restless all the time. I'd much rather be doing something like this. I can't quite believe I've reached the age of thirty-six and not visited London before. I said to Mother, "I've reached the age of thirty-six and I've never visited London before." And so she said to me I must simply go. And it's only two hours on the train. Isn't it silly having never visited when it's only two hours on the train? Mother didn't want to come with me because she's too infirm these days. It started off with a pain in her back, but now it's spread to her hip. And it's travelling down her leg, too. She's seen the doctor lots of times about it, but he doesn't seem able to help.'

'I'm sorry to hear it.'

'It's getting to the stage now where she can't even walk to the shops. So I'm having to do errands for her. Obviously I'm worrying about her while I'm here in London, but our neighbour is going to look after her for a few days. I promised Mother I would buy some postcards for her. Will there be a place to buy postcards in Richmond-upon-Thames?'

'I expect so.'

The river was busy with other pleasure boats as well as barges and vessels which served the wharves and warehouses along the riverside.

'Oh, look, we're coming up to another bridge,' said Jennifer. 'How many bridges are there over the Thames?'

'A lot,' said Augusta. 'I can't remember the exact number.'

'I wish now that I'd begun counting them from when we first left. There was one very near the jetty, wasn't there?'

'That one was Westminster Bridge.'

'And then there was... I've forgotten the name of it now.'

'Lambeth Bridge,' said Augusta.

'And this one?'

'Vauxhall Bridge.'

'How pretty.'

Although Augusta knew London well, she rarely saw the city from the river. She was enjoying the different vantage point. She would have enjoyed it more if she didn't have Cousin Jennifer for company.

'Mother gets such terrible headaches. I think it's all because of some tooth pain she had about six months ago. I kept telling her to see the dentist about it, but she refused! She was worried the dentist was going to pull the tooth right out of her head. Well, we all know that's not very pleasant, is it? But I told her it was better than having to endure such awful pain. But she wouldn't listen to me. And now the pain has spread to other parts of her head.'

There was a pause as Augusta attempted to find a suitable response. 'Does she still have the tooth pain?' she eventually asked.

'No, it's moved to other parts of her head. She takes headache powders for it, but I don't think they're doing her much good. She's been seeing the doctor about her pains in her back and hip and leg. I've told her to mention the headaches as well, but she's worried he'll think she's making a fuss. And as he's not really done much about the other pains, I can't imagine that he'll do much about the head pains either. It's not very easy getting old.'

'How old is she?'

'Fifty-five. I'm worried she won't make it to sixty.'

Augusta glanced around at the other passengers, wondering if any would be willing to join the conversation. She was struggling to endure it alone. But everyone else seemed busy admiring the view and discussing it with their companions.

'I can see two bridges coming up!' said Jennifer.

'Victoria Bridge, which is a railway bridge, and Chelsea Bridge.'

'Chelsea! I've heard of that. I should like to visit

Chelsea while I'm in London, but I don't think I'll find enough time. There's so much to see and do here, isn't there?'

'There certainly is.'

'Where do you live, Augusta?'

'In Bloomsbury.'

'I've heard of that too! You must be very rich.'

Augusta smiled as she thought of her little flat above the tailor's shop in scruffy Marchmont Street. 'No, I'm not rich at all.'

'I refuse to believe it. You must be richer than me and Mother. We're just simple country folk.'

'As were my family,' said Augusta.

'Is that a park?' said Jennifer.

'It looks like one.'

'London has so many parks, doesn't it? I really thought it would all be dirty fog and smoke. But only parts of it are like that, aren't they? The rest of London is quite pretty.'

'Some of it is,' said Augusta. 'And some of it is not pretty at all.'

'It's certainly more interesting than Westbury,' said Jennifer, referring to the town nearest to her Wiltshire home. 'But there is a pretty park in Westbury which Mother and I like to walk in.'

Augusta stopped listening to Jennifer as her eye was drawn to a small rowing boat bobbing in the water close by. There was no one in it and it appeared to be adrift. Perhaps it had come loose from its moorings somewhere, but it could presumably cause a problem for the river traffic.

She peered closely at the little boat as they passed close by. There was something in it. A canvas sheet draped over a bundle.

Augusta knelt on the seat and leaned forward to look

before the little boat passed by. The spray from the river was damp on her face.

And then she saw it.

A tendril of dark hair was visible just beneath the edge of the canvas.

An icy shiver ran through her. Something didn't feel right.

'Stop the boat!' she called out.

Chapter 5

'AS SOON AS I saw the dark hair, I knew there had to be someone lying beneath that tarpaulin,' said Augusta with a shiver. She stood with Fred and Philip in her shop.

'Presumably the river police were quick to arrive,' said Philip.

Augusta nodded. 'Within minutes. The captain of the pleasure boat called them on his radio for help and they got there very quickly. We found out it was a woman in the boat, but that was all. I had hoped she was still alive and could recover with some medical assistance, but…' She paused as she felt a heavy sadness in her chest. 'I suppose there was little chance she was going to be alive, was there? No one would choose to float adrift on the river covered in tarpaulin.'

'I'm surprised someone didn't spot the boat sooner,' said Philip.

'Me too, the river is always busy. Too busy to notice a little rowboat drifting alone, perhaps? It put an end to our day trip. Many people on the boat were quite upset, and the captain decided to return to Westminster Pier.'

'That's understandable,' said Fred. 'What happened to Cousin Jennifer?'

'She was horrified. As soon as we landed at Westminster, she took a taxi to collect her things from the hotel and then onto Paddington railway station.'

'She's gone home?'

'Yes. Back to Westbury. The incident on the river frightened her away.'

'I never got to meet her,' said Philip.

'You didn't miss much.'

'Oh dear, was she not very good company?'

'I found her conversation a little tiring. But that's probably my fault. I'm not very good at small talk and I think I'm rather fussy about who I keep company with. Anyway, I'm more concerned about the poor woman who was found in the boat. I wonder how easy it will be to find out who she was.'

'That's something for my former colleagues at Scotland Yard to deal with,' said Philip. 'Although I must admit, I'm rather interested in the case.'

'But you can no longer be involved.'

'No. I've left all that now. So we shall just have to watch from the sidelines and find out how the case progresses.'

'If you hadn't left Scotland Yard, Philip, you could be working on this case at this very moment,' said Fred.

'True. And this is exactly the sort of case I enjoyed investigating. But I had my reasons for leaving and I have to remember them.'

Philip had been replaced on a recent case by the Commissioner's inexperienced son and the experience had left him disillusioned with his work.

'Perhaps you might be involved in this case, after all?' said Fred. 'It might become so complicated that Scotland Yard needs your help.'

Philip laughed. 'I think it would have to be very difficult indeed for any of my former colleagues to come asking for help!'

'I wonder how long she was in the boat for,' said Augusta. 'It can't have been for very long, otherwise someone would surely have spotted her sooner. And where did the boat enter the water? That section of the Thames is tidal, so the boat could have moved some distance either east or west.'

'It's going to be difficult to work out where the boat entered the water,' said Philip. 'The police surgeon will be able to provide a good guess at the time of death and perhaps the river police will be able to look at what the tide was doing at that time and work out where the boat could have come from. My guess is the boat went into the water last night. If the poor woman was murdered, then the culprit is more likely to do it under the cover of darkness, aren't they?'

'You think it could be murder?' said Augusta.

'It's not a nice thought. But how else can it be explained?'

Chapter 6

FRED WAS READING the newspaper at the counter when Augusta arrived at her shop the following morning.

'Is there a report on the lady in the boat?' she asked as she placed Sparky's cage on the counter. She looked after the canary for her elderly friend, Lady Hereford. Sparky accompanied her home every evening and joined her in the shop every day.

'I'm reading about it now,' said Fred. 'Her name was Ellen Foster, and she was a news reporter for the *London Weekly Chronicle*.'

'A news reporter?'

'Apparently, her colleagues are extremely upset.'

'I'm not surprised.'

'Here's a picture of her.'

The photograph showed a young woman with a fine-boned face surrounded by a cloud of dark hair. She had keen, intelligent eyes and a thin mouth.

I wonder if her profession had anything to do with her death?'

'You think she might have upset someone?'

'It's a possibility. Maybe she was investigating someone who didn't appreciate her attention.'

'News reporters can be unpopular with some people, can't they?'

'Yes. And particularly unpopular with people who have something to hide. I wonder what she was investigating. We can't be completely sure that the job was the reason for her death, but it certainly makes it a possibility.'

'I suppose the police already have an idea about that. The editor would have told them what she was working on, and perhaps they've got a lead from that.'

'It's very sad. Does the news article say how old she was?'

'She was thirty.'

'I suppose another possibility is a violent husband,' said Augusta.

'It says here that she wasn't married.'

'A boyfriend, perhaps? But a violent partner can be an easy suspect, and I would have thought the police would have either made an arrest or stated they were looking for him.'

'I agree,' said Fred. 'Sometimes an unpleasant chap does something like that, then runs off and the police have to find him. But if the culprit had been a violent boyfriend, then why was Miss Foster murdered in a boat?'

'Good question. I think if a boyfriend were to carry out such a thing, it's more likely to have taken place in or near their homes. Perhaps I'm wrong because I don't know the details of the case. But murder in a boat is strange, isn't it?'

'Apparently she was shot.'

'How awful! And you'd have thought someone would have heard gunshots. Sounds that loud would carry across the water, so someone on the riverside or in another boat must have heard it. Especially if the attack was carried out at night.'

'They believe it was. When the boat was found drifting, they don't think it had been in the water for any longer than twelve hours.'

'So someone decided to shoot Ellen Foster in a boat late at night and then leave her to be found the next day,' said Augusta. She shuddered. 'Unbelievably cold-hearted and cruel.'

'I wonder if she was attacked in the boat?' said Fred. 'Or was she harmed elsewhere then put in the boat?'

'If she had been attacked in the boat while on the water, then the culprit would have had to leave the boat. They could have clambered onto another boat, but it would have had to have been alongside the little rowing boat. Or maybe they swam to the riverbank? That's a brave thing to do in a cold, filthy river with strong tidal currents.'

'You'd have to be a confident swimmer.'

'You would.' Augusta picked up the bag of bird seed and fed some seeds to Sparky. 'For the time being, it's a mystery. And I can only wonder how the police are getting on with it.'

Chapter 7

AUGUSTA SPENT the first part of the morning in her workshop. A mistreated copy of *The Moonstone* by Wilkie Collins tested her mending skills. It was an attractive edition with an emerald green cover and gold embossed embellishments. The cover had become detached, and the spine was damaged. Augusta leafed through the book and determined it still had all of its pages. As long as a book had all its pages, there was hope she could restore it.

She had been working for a while when she heard Philip's voice beyond the door. In need of a break, she decided to go into the shop and find out what he and Fred were discussing.

'Hello Augusta,' said Philip. To her surprise, he was accompanied by an attractive lady with large blue eyes, dark bobbed hair and rosebud lips. She wore a lilac coat over a matching dress, and her fashionable cloche hat had a sprig of fresh flowers tucked into the hatband. She looked like a lady who enjoyed spending time on her appearance. 'This is Mrs Dashwood,' continued Philip. 'My first client.'

'It's nice to meet you, Mrs Dashwood,' said Augusta. She attempted to brush away the disappointment that Philip's first client was an attractive lady about ten years her junior.

'I've been telling Mrs Dashwood all about your shop,' said Philip. 'So I suggested to her that we come down here and have a look around.'

'I love bookshops,' said Mrs Dashwood. Her voice was soft with perfect diction. 'I particularly like second-hand books. They have so much character, don't they? And older books are so beautifully made. Mr Fisher tells me you repair these books yourself, Mrs Peel.'

'That's right. I like to give them a second chance.'

'You're very skilled indeed.'

'I don't know about that,' said Augusta. 'I think I probably just feel sorry for old books. I don't like to see them being thrown away.'

'Augusta once repaired an old book of mine from my childhood,' said Philip.

'Did you indeed, Mrs Peel? How very clever. I wish I was skilled with my hands.'

'It's a skill which anybody can learn,' Augusta said.

'Is that so? Maybe I shall try when…' Her expression fell, and she gave a little sniff.

'Mrs Dashwood is going through a torrid time,' said Philip. 'Her husband has gone missing.'

'Goodness, how awful!' said Fred.

'I'm so sorry to hear it, Mrs Dashwood,' said Augusta.

'The police are being hopeless about it,' said Mrs Dashwood. 'And that's why I've consulted Mr Fisher.'

'When did you last see your husband?' asked Augusta.

'It was at breakfast time, two mornings ago. Leonard went to work as usual, but he never came home. I know he went to work because his colleagues told me he did. And he left work at the usual time and was seen walking in the direction of Charing Cross tube station. That was the last time anyone saw him.'

'Terrible,' said Fred, shaking his head.

'I take it your husband hasn't gone missing before?' said Augusta.

'No, never. It's completely out of character. There was nothing bothering him as far as I was aware. We've been perfectly happily married for six years. I don't understand how he can vanish like this. The police asked me if he'd been having an affair! Can you believe it? It was most upsetting. I told them he hadn't because I'd have known about it. And they said he'll probably turn up again before long. They told me he can look after himself. They suggested that maybe he wanted to go away for a few days, and that he has every right to do so without telling anybody where he is. I can see that point, but I know my husband. I know he would never do such a thing.'

'I think you are the best judge of whether to be worried or not,' said Augusta. 'I suppose the police are very busy, and they don't consider him to be at risk. But you know him better than anyone, and if you're worried, then I think it was a good idea to consult Philip. He will do everything to help.'

'I certainly will,' said Philip. 'And it won't do any harm to give some of my former colleagues a bit of a talking to about this. Although they're clearly not worried about Mr Dashwood, he could have come to some harm, and I think they should be doing something. They haven't done anything at all.'

'I've telephoned all the hospitals I know of,' said Mrs Dashwood. 'I thought maybe he'd had an accident and banged his head and suffered memory loss or something.

But there's nobody matching his description who's been admitted to any of the hospitals recently.'

'But we'll keep trying with that,' said Philip. 'It's possible he's been admitted somewhere. We'll find him, Mrs Dashwood.'

'Thank you, Mr Fisher.' She flashed him a smile and patted him on the arm. 'You're such a comfort at this difficult time.'

Chapter 8

LADY HEREFORD VISITED THAT AFTERNOON. Her nurse wheeled her bath chair into the shop and positioned her by Sparky's cage on the counter.

'I have some apple for you today, Sparky,' said the old lady. 'But before I give it to you, I need to hear from Augusta that you've been behaving yourself.'

'Of course he has,' said Augusta. 'He always behaves himself.'

'Good.' Lady Hereford used a fruit knife to cut a small piece from an apple and passed it to Sparky through the door of his cage.

'Sparky's very excited about our new neighbour,' said Augusta.

'Oh yes, Detective Inspector Fisher from the Yard! He's moved in now, has he?'

'Yes. And he's just plain Mr Fisher now.'

'What a shame. Detective Inspector sounds so much better. Does he have any clients yet?'

'One.'

'Only one?'

'He's just opened for business in the past few days.'

'I suppose it's the sort of job where one has to earn a reputation for oneself. Being a former detective of Scotland Yard should stand him in good stead, but people need to know about his services, don't they? Has he been advertising?'

'Yes, he's put advertisements in the newspapers.'

'A lot of private detectives get involved in divorce cases these days. With divorce becoming ever more popular, they're being employed to follow people about and catch them with someone who's not their spouse. Let's hope he doesn't have too many of those cases. I can imagine they must be very boring to work on. His skills would be quite lost on such work. Sparky's enjoying this apple, isn't he? You can't have too much of it though, Sparky. Treats can only be given in small amounts.' She turned back to Augusta. 'I think it's a shame Mr Fisher left the Yard. I think his skills are needed for this terrible case of the murdered news reporter who was found floating in a boat on the Thames. What a tragedy. And what a strange crime! I hope they catch the person who did it. I don't suppose you've heard anything more about it, have you?'

'I saw the rowing boat adrift on the river,' said Augusta, 'but other than that, I don't know any more details than have been reported in the newspapers.'

'Just a moment, Augusta. Did you just say you saw the boat in which the poor lady was found?'

'Yes. It was awful. Fortunately, the river police were on the scene quickly.'

'Yes, I expect they were. It always astonishes me, Augusta, how you bump into these cases.'

'I'd rather not bump into them.'

'You might be able to solve this one.'

'There's no need for me to do any work on it, Lady

Hereford. Scotland Yard is investigating and I don't think they need Philip or me to help them.'

'Well, I suppose they know where to find you if they do. I can imagine it must be quite dangerous to be a news reporter. Especially if you're reporting on someone who's up to no good. I can only imagine that's what has happened in this case. The poor young woman probably wrote an article about someone and they took objection to it. Murdering her like that is no way to solve it, of course. I suppose they've done it as a deterrent to other news reporters. It would be interesting to find out what she was working on.'

'Yes, it would be interesting to find out. But her death could have had nothing to do with her job, it could have been something else entirely.'

'Yes, I suppose so. It's rather frustrating that Mr Fisher no longer works for Scotland Yard. If he did, then we would know everything, wouldn't we? But instead, we just have to find out what we can from the newspapers.'

Chapter 9

LADY HEREFORD'S comment gave Augusta an idea. After the old lady had left, Augusta asked Fred to mind the shop while she paid a visit to Holborn Library.

The walk took less than ten minutes and Augusta enjoyed the shortcut through Bloomsbury Square, where birds sang from trees with fresh spring leaves.

At the library, Augusta made her way to the newspaper archive. The *London Weekly Chronicle* wasn't a newspaper she often read, but she hoped that browsing its past editions might tell her more about Ellen Foster.

She made herself comfortable at a desk with a pile of recent editions and began to look through them. There were too many advertisements for her liking, but she felt fortunate it was a weekly publication. A daily newspaper would have meant many more papers to look through.

There was no sign of the name Ellen Foster. Only a few of the articles had by-lines and often the terms "staff reporter" or "our news reporter" were used. As Augusta scanned local events, political news and book reviews, she found little that could offend someone.

Then she came across a report about an accident at a tin box factory in Deptford. An interview with an unnamed employee at the factory claimed a recent accident had not been reported to His Majesty's Factory Inspectorate. The employee also claimed it was a dangerous factory to work in and that several other accidents hadn't been reported when they were required to be.

As Augusta looked through more editions, she realised a series of articles had been written about the factory. One reported that the owner of the factory, James Stevenson, had previously been fined for two accidents where workers had lost fingers while operating the power press machines. Another article suggested accidents were being covered up so Stevenson could avoid further fines. Some injured workers had reportedly been paid to leave their employment and keep quiet about their ordeal. Augusta grew queasy after reading reports of amputated fingers and arms. One report listed all the accidents which had occurred at the factory over the previous five years. Augusta knew little about the Factory Act, but she knew there were rules in place to ensure workers were kept safe. Factories these days had much better working conditions than in the previous century, but the catalogue of incidents at the factory suggested many workers were at the mercy of poor management.

There was no indication who the reports were written by, but they were just the sort of thing which would anger the factory owner. One article stated attempts had been made to contact James Stevenson, but he had refused to speak to the newspaper.

If Ellen Foster had written the articles, then perhaps James Stevenson had wished her to be silenced? Augusta could see a motive, but she couldn't yet prove that Ellen

Foster had written the articles or that James Stevenson had anything to do with her death.

She sat back in her chair and sighed. All she could do was speculate. And there had been no need for her to come to the library and spend a few hours looking over past editions of the *Weekly Chronicle*. The case was being worked on by Philip's former colleagues at Scotland Yard. Even Philip wasn't involved.

But Augusta had seen poor Ellen Foster in the boat. That's why she couldn't forget about the case. She wanted to see the perpetrator caught. She tried to reassure herself that Scotland Yard would follow this line of inquiry. She could only hope the detectives had spoken to the editor of the *Weekly Chronicle*, and he had told them what Ellen Foster had been working on.

Who was James Stevenson? Augusta consulted several directories, hoping to find mention of him. She couldn't find his name, but in *Who's Who* she found a Jonathan Stevenson. He had died three years ago and had owned factories across London and the Midlands. Could he have been a relation? Augusta knew the perfect person to ask.

Chapter 10

'JONATHAN STEVENSON,' Lady Hereford mused over the name the following morning. Augusta was visiting her in the suite of rooms she occupied on the fourth floor of the Russell Hotel. Lady Hereford had lived there since the death of her husband, having sold their home. The day room was scented with rose water and filled with vases of flowers. Augusta and Lady Hereford sat in two chairs by a tall window overlooking the greenery of Russell Square.

'Stevenson was a wealthy man,' said Lady Hereford. 'He inherited the business from his father and expanded it. I met him once at a dinner hosted by the Lord Mayor of London at Mansion House. He married a quiet girl from a very old family. The Addenbrookes. Stevenson was pleasant enough, a little brusque perhaps. A lot of these chaps who run businesses often are these days. They get carried away with the relentless pace of their work and forget their manners sometimes.'

'Was one of his factories in Deptford?'

'Possibly. I can't be certain, though. Like I say, I only met him once, and I didn't ask him a great deal about his factories because factories simply aren't interesting, are they? Very necessary, of course. But they make for a dull conversation topic.'

'The newspaper which the murdered reporter Ellen Foster worked for published a series of articles about accidents at a tin box factory in Deptford,' said Augusta. 'Apparently the owner of the factory is James Stevenson.'

'James Stevenson? Interesting. Possibly a son of Jonathan Stevenson then. And I recall something about tin boxes now. I'm quite sure that was the line of business the Stevensons were in. How did you find out about the news articles, Augusta?'

'I read some recent copies of the *London Weekly Chronicle.*'

'That's quite dedicated of you considering you're not even working on the case. I can see how articles about accidents at one of the Stevenson factories could be unpopular with the family.'

'I don't know if Ellen Foster wrote the articles, though.'

'The editor of the newspaper would be able to tell you. Although you'd have to find a legitimate reason for speaking to him about it. And if you're not officially working on the case, then that could be tricky. I can't imagine James Stevenson harming a reporter in revenge, though. I would have thought the commonplace thing to do would be to make a complaint to the editor.'

'I agree,' said Augusta. 'Perhaps it's just a far-fetched idea of mine. I suppose I'm trying to look for a reason why someone would murder Ellen Foster.'

'I don't know the Stevenson family well, but I can ask around for you. I'm sure some friends will be able to tell me a little more about them.' Lady Hereford gave a smile. 'You can't help yourself, can you, Augusta?'

'What do you mean?'

'You could be quietly repairing books and running your shop. But instead you've begun investigating this tragic case.'

'I haven't begun investigating,' said Augusta, realising she was quickly leaping to her own defence. 'I'm just… interested.'

'If you say so.'

'And when I realised there was someone under that tarpaulin in that boat…' Augusta shuddered at the memory. 'I suppose I want to do something about it. I know I should leave it to Scotland Yard. But what if they miss a clue?'

Chapter 11

JAMES STEVENSON TRIED to make himself comfortable in the car, but the ride was too uncomfortable. They needed to fix the holes in London's roads. Or were the car's tyres to blame?

'Smith!' he called out to his driver in front of him.

'Sir?'

'When did you last check the tyres?'

'This morning, sir.'

'This ride is very bumpy. Perhaps you can check them again?'

'I shall see to it, sir.'

James rested his head back and gazed out of the window at the people bustling along Regent Street. The sunshine made his head ache and his mouth felt dry and sour. He wasn't good in the mornings. Grimston had no doubt arranged a morning meeting just to spite him.

And James was probably still drunk. He hadn't got to bed until five. Rita Crawford had hosted an Arabian Nights themed party. Everyone had been there, but he couldn't remember anything that had happened after midnight. He had probably said some foolish things again which he would be reminded of the next time he saw his friends.

Smith steered the car right into Pall Mall and pulled up outside Grimston's office. It was in a five-storey building with an ornate stone facade and a shiny black door.

James lounged in his seat as he waited for Smith to get out of the car, walk around the back, and open the door for him.

'Thank you, Smith,' he said as he clambered out. His head spun a little as he stood up straight. 'Don't forget to check those tyres.'

'YOU KNOW I HATE MORNING MEETINGS,' said James as he sank into a high-backed leather chair in Mr Grimston's office.

'The morning is the best part of the day, sir. And the most productive.' Grimston was a lean man with silver framed spectacles and thinning grey hair. He had looked after the business affairs of the Stevenson family for thirty years and James had never seen him wear anything other than a smart black suit. Life had changed a lot over the past three decades, but Grimston still looked the same.

'Whoever decided that mornings are the most productive time of day clearly doesn't know me,' said James. He lit a cigarette and gazed out of the window while Grimston updated him on the business. Expenditure was up, income was down, and something would have to be done about it.

'You know what I think about it all,' he said, once Grimston had finished droning on. 'We just need to sell the business.'

'Your father stipulated it should not be sold.'

James sighed. The old man was dead. What did it matter now?

'And your brother—'

'Yes, I know my brother doesn't want the business to be sold, either. But that's irrelevant. I'm the eldest son and I inherited it, not him.'

'Everyone in the family has an interest in the business. You cannot simply do as you wish with it, sir.'

Tin boxes. His family had been manufacturing them for nearly eighty years. He had lost count of the times he had been bored by the story of how tin boxes had made his family's fortune. His father had even made him work in one of the factories for a week when he was fourteen years old. James had hated every minute of it and had rarely set foot in any of the factories since.

'There is little doubt that production could be a little more efficient,' said Mr Grimston. 'I think staff numbers could be cut without too much detriment to production.'

'Well, let's do that then,' said James.

'For all six factories?'

'I don't know. Which factory is the least efficient?'

'Deptford.'

'That one then.'

'I don't believe it's as simple as that, sir. Morale is already low at Deptford. If we reduce staff numbers there, then production will fall much further. Until the problems in Deptford are resolved, I propose we cut the staff numbers at a factory where the staff will more readily take on extra work.'

'I'm happy to go with what you suggest, Grimston.'

'Of course, sir.' He made some notes in a jotter in front of him. 'I shall look at the five other factories and advise a course of action. In the meantime, we should feel relieved that the *London Weekly Chronicle* will leave us alone now.'

'Will they? Why?'

'Have you not heard about the death of their news reporter?'

'No. Someone died?'

'You must have heard about the murdered young woman who was found in the boat on the Thames. It was Ellen Foster, the reporter who had been making quite a bit of trouble for us.'

'The lady in the boat? I read about it. She was the news reporter? Gosh, I didn't realise that. Very sad.'

'You do know what she had been writing about the Deptford factory, don't you, sir?'

'Of course. I just didn't realise it was her who was found in the boat. That's terribly bad luck. She must have upset someone, I suppose.'

'I'd say she did, sir. But we don't need to worry about her anymore.'

'Well, that's excellent news. Rather sad, but hopefully, it will put a stop to the news articles. All this fuss about accidents. Every factory has accidents. I don't understand why they decided to pick on us.'

'Me neither. And you'll also be pleased to hear that we found the employee who had been talking to Miss Foster.'

'Well done, Grimston. Has the employee been punished?'

'Very much so.'

'Good. I don't know why someone would complain to a reporter about their employer. They must have been paid a decent sum of money, I suppose. But whatever happened to loyalty?'

'My sentiment exactly, sir. Some money will have

changed hands and the employee would have told Miss Foster whatever she wanted to hear. Most of it nonsense too.'

'I'd say. I'm pleased it's all been sorted now. Thank you, Grimston.'

Chapter 12

'THERE'S STILL no sign of Mr Dashwood,' said Philip. 'It's been three days now. I'm in regular contact with all the main hospitals and Metropolitan Police divisions, but there's no news at all. It's as if he's vanished into thin air.'

'He was last seen heading for Charing Cross tube station?' asked Augusta.

'That's right. He travelled every day on the Hampstead Tube between his home in Tufnell Park and Charing Cross. He was a man of habit and never made a detour on his way home in the evenings. He was always back by half-past six without fail. Mrs Dashwood is beside herself with worry.'

'I'm not surprised. It's very puzzling. Do you think there's a possibility he chose to leave his wife?'

'He could have done and obviously I'm careful about discussing that possibility with Mrs Dashwood because the thought is extremely upsetting to her. But from what I've learned of his character, I really don't think he would have done such a thing. I've spoken to just about everyone who knows him. Friends, family and colleagues.'

'Perhaps he has a secret side to him?'

'I should think it's unlikely. If he has, then perhaps we have no hope of finding him. Unfortunately, I think it's most likely he's come to harm. He could have been attacked and robbed and left for dead somewhere.'

'But surely someone would have found him by now?' said Fred.

'True.' Philip nodded. 'It really is baffling. Anyway, I shall take a break from thinking about it and find myself a book to read.' He walked over to the bookshelves.

'And what do you like the look of?' asked Augusta.

'This book of Sherlock Holmes stories.' He took it off the shelf. 'I think I've read some of these before, but I'm sure I'll enjoy them again. I may even buy a deerstalker hat and a pipe. And perhaps I could get myself a violin too. Do you think that would put your customers off?'

'It will if you don't know how to play it.'

'I don't, I'm afraid. How much do I owe you for the book?'

'You don't.'

'No Augusta, I insist on paying for it.'

'It's a gift. To celebrate the opening of your detective agency this week. You can pay me for the next book you like the look of.'

'Very well. Thank you for the gift, Augusta.'

The telephone rang.

'Let me get that,' said Philip. 'It could be Mrs Dashwood.'

Augusta tried to ignore her disappointment when Philip turned out to be right. The conversation seemed light and convivial, even though they were discussing a missing husband.

Perhaps it was all a ruse and Mrs Dashwood had murdered him? Augusta pushed the uncharitable thought from her mind.

It was Ellen Foster's murder which needed solving, and she had an idea about how to speak with someone at the *London Weekly Chronicle*. She turned to Fred. 'I'm wondering if I can ask a favour from your friend, Boris.'

'What sort of favour?' Fred looked puzzled.

'I would like to borrow Titus for a couple of hours.'

Chapter 13

EARLY THAT EVENING, Augusta took Titus for a walk along Fleet Street. The little dog pulled on the lead, keen to greet everyone who passed by. He wasn't fussy about who he approached and appeared to happily assume that people were as pleased to see him as he was to see them.

It was the time of day when news reporters were leaving their offices and heading for either the railway station or a pub. Augusta strolled back and forth by the *London Weekly Chronicle* offices. Hopefully, a reporter from the newspaper would emerge before long and Titus could make an introduction.

Augusta wanted to find out if Ellen Foster had written the articles about the Stevenson factory. And she also wanted to learn more about Ellen Foster. She could only hope she would bump into someone helpful from the *Weekly Chronicle*.

The door to the offices opened and a man with a neat red moustache hurried out. Fortunately, he walked in Augusta's direction. She allowed Titus's lead to lengthen for a moment and readied herself to pass him.

Within seconds, Titus had launched himself at the man's shins.

'Oi! Get off you little rascal!'

Augusta pulled the dog away before the man could knock him with his briefcase. 'Oh, goodness, I'm so sorry,' she said. 'He's a little too friendly, and I wasn't paying attention.'

'You need to keep a better eye on him on a busy street like this.' He gave her a sharp glare. His wide-set eyes were pale green with no hint of friendliness in them. He bent down and brushed his trousers as if Titus had soiled them. Augusta could see no sign of dirt.

'I do apologise,' she said. 'It was a short lapse in concentration. I hope he hasn't damaged your trousers?'

'No. No harm done. But it's bad manners to allow your dog to do such a thing.'

'I'm aware of that and I'm terribly sorry.' She glanced up at the sign on the building, as if she had only just noticed it for the first time. 'The *London Weekly Chronicle*,' she said. 'I read the sad story about your reporter, Miss Foster.'

'Indeed. It's been very upsetting for us.'

'You were one of her colleagues?'

'I was.'

'You're also a reporter on the *Weekly Chronicle*?'

'Yes. Walter Ferguson.'

'It's nice to meet you, Mr Ferguson. My name is Augusta Peel. I was so terribly saddened to read about your colleague's death. Has anyone got any idea who could have been behind it?'

'None at all. It's in the hands of Scotland Yard.'

'Could her murder have had something to do with her work?'

'I sincerely hope not. Otherwise, we could all be in trouble.'

'I'm a regular reader of the *Weekly Chronicle*.'

'Are you?'

'Yes. And I know that sometimes you publish articles which investigate injustice. The accidents at the Stevensons' tin box factory in Deptford, for example.'

His eyes narrowed a little. 'We like to pride ourselves on investigative reporting, as we call it. And the factory report has been one of our recent campaigns. The *Weekly Chronicle* has a proud history of investigating local issues and not everyone takes kindly to it. But it's impossible to imagine one of our reporters would be murdered over it. If that could be the case, then I would have to resign my position at this very moment.'

'Was Miss Foster working on the Deptford factory articles?'

'Yes, she was. Her death wouldn't have had anything to do with her work, though. Miss Foster was a colleague for four years, and I respected her a great deal. I knew little about her personal affairs and I can only imagine the reason for her death is a private matter. Scotland Yard will get to the bottom of it, I'm sure.' He checked his watch. 'I really must be going. Good day to you, Mrs Peel. And keep your dog under control.'

Chapter 14

WALTER FERGUSON STEPPED into The Old Bell pub feeling a little shaken. There had been something odd about Mrs Peel, and he couldn't put his finger on it. She had keen, intelligent eyes, as if she knew exactly what she wanted. Was it possible she had been waiting for him outside the newspaper offices? But if that was the case, how did she know who he was and where he would be?

Her questions about Ellen Foster's death had been quite direct. Why did she want to know about Ellen? Although he could understand the interest in Ellen's tragic death, he couldn't understand why a middle-aged, auburn-haired lady with an annoying dog would question him directly about it.

Perhaps she was just strange.

He leaned against the bar and ordered a whisky and a pint of London porter.

The sooner everyone stopped talking about Ellen, the better. He and his colleagues had been interviewed at great length by the police. He could only hope an arrest would be made soon, then speculation about Ellen's death would stop. But the police were taking their time. Surely they could round up the usual collection of criminal types? The most likely culprit could be plucked from the group and persuaded to confess. Wasn't that the way the police usually dealt with these things?

He swigged down his whisky and was joined at the bar by an old friend, John Ramsden of *The London News*.

'Any word on any arrests yet?'

'No. And it's not surprising when you consider who's in charge.'

'That young Detective Sergeant?'

Walter nodded. 'Joyce. The Commissioner's son.'

'I wonder why he got the job, then?' John cackled and ordered a drink from the barmaid.

'He's barely old enough to be out of short trousers,' said Walter.

'Any ideas on who did it?'

'None. You know what Ellen was like, she always had several stories on the go. She clearly upset someone, and they had their revenge.'

'Very worrying. I know we're not popular people, but we don't deserve to be murdered for our work.'

'No, we don't. But I don't think you and I have got anything to worry about.'

'Why not?'

'We're men. It's much easier for us to fight off an attacker. Ellen was a woman and therefore vulnerable. This is what happens when women get involved in a man's world. You and I both know that. We've both been threatened.'

John nodded. 'We have.' He took a gulp of porter and spilt some down his front.

'Ellen put herself at risk. She wanted to do the sort of work a man does, but she didn't appreciate the danger involved and she paid the ultimate price. It's very sad, but she took risks.'

'I suppose we all take risks.' John wiped the dribble of porter from the waistcoat stretched over his belly.

'Yes, we do. But you and I can look after ourselves, can't we? For a woman, it's not so easy. And it's not looking good for the *Weekly Chronicle* now.'

'Why not?'

'The editor's devastated about Ellen's death. You know he always carried a torch for her?'

'Did he?'

'It wasn't reciprocated. But he adored her. You should see him now. He's pale, unshaven, and barely knows what day it is. He's in no fit state to work at the moment.'

'He was in love with her?'

'Probably. He always gave her the best stories.'

'That's favouritism.' John lit his pipe.

'It is. And it's wrong.'

'She was good at what she did, though, wasn't she?'

'She was alright. For a woman. But it would have been better if she'd stuck to women's topics. Fashion, cookery, that sort of thing. Instead, she wanted the stories the rest of us were working on. And the editor, Baker, gave them to her. People like you and me lost out.'

'Not me.' John blew out a puff of smoke. 'I write for the *London News*.'

'What I mean is reporters like us. Men who've been working on Fleet Street for years and know what we're doing. You immediately create a problem when you bring women into the workplace. Emotions come into play. There's favouritism and infatuation. It skews everything.'

'Well, she's gone now, Walter, so you don't need to worry about it anymore.'

'It's the questions though, isn't it? The police questioned us all for hours yesterday, it was almost impossible to get any work done. You worry they're pointing the finger at you.'

'I wouldn't worry about that. They need evidence first.'

'But it's other people, too. A strange lady with a horrible little dog questioned me about Ellen earlier. She claimed to have been passing by, but I'm not sure she was. It felt like she'd sought me out. She told me her name was Augusta Peel. Have you heard of her?'

'No.'

Walter took a sip of porter. 'I think she's up to something.'

Chapter 15

LADY HEREFORD TELEPHONED the following day.

'Augusta, I've done a little asking around about the Stevensons. I've discovered that a good friend of mine, Lady Arbuthnot, knew Jonathan Stevenson. She's not particularly impressed with his heir, James, however.'

'Why not?'

'By all accounts, he's young and feckless. He's inherited six factories from his father, but doesn't have any interest in any of them. Apparently, he leaves all the day-to-day running of them to an old employee of the family firm. He spends a lot of his time partying with these bright young people, or whatever they're called these days. A bit of a hedonist, it's said.'

'So he's not a businessman at all?'

'He doesn't seem to be. That's what Lady Arbuthnot says, anyway. Apparently, he spends most of his time at parties with writers, artists, photographers, actors, and actresses, you name it. All the fashionable people. There are two sisters who seem to be at the centre of it all, Rita and Bridget Crawford. I knew their mother. I'm not sure what the sisters do other than spend money and go to parties, but I've seen photographs of them in the society magazine, *Aristo*. They're rather beautiful, which I suppose counts for everything these days. It's astonishing, isn't it, how people can become so well-known for doing so little? Anyway, from what I hear about the sisters, they seem to party with just about anybody as long as they're rich and attractive. Awfully superficial, if you ask me.'

'Do you recall seeing photographs of James Stevenson in *Aristo*?' asked Augusta.

'No, but that's probably because he's not as eye-catching as the sisters. And he seems quite ill-suited to be in charge of a large business.'

'So he's not got any interest in the accidents happening in his Deptford factory.'

'I assume not.'

'And if he's as disinterested as he sounds, then presumably he's not too upset about what the *Weekly Chronicle* has published.'

'Possibly not. But I can't speak for him, Augusta. I don't know him.'

Augusta thanked her and replaced the telephone receiver.

'I couldn't help overhearing,' said Fred. 'But did you mention the magazine *Aristo*?'

'Yes. Do you read it?'

'I do, I'm afraid.'

'Fred!' Augusta smiled. 'I didn't realise you enjoy society magazines.'

'My mother subscribes. And when she's finished reading it each week, I'm afraid I pick it up and read it too.'

'So you've read about Rita and Bridget Crawford?'

'Yes! They're the girls of the moment. They get a mention at least once in every edition.'

'Apparently James Stevenson, the owner of the factory Ellen Foster wrote about, likes to party with them. From what you've read about the two sisters, Fred, what can you tell me about them?'

'They're from an aristocratic Scottish family. Rita likes to write and has been a muse for various artists and photographers. Bridget is an actress, although I don't think she works very often. She likes to paint.'

'And go to parties from the sound of things.'

'They're always at parties.'

'Do you have any old copies of *Aristo*?'

'Yes, lots!'

'Would you mind bringing them in? I would like to see if James Stevenson gets mention in there. I want to learn as much about him as possible, and *Aristo* seems a good place to start.'

'I'll look through them for you, Augusta, and let you know what I find.'

'Thank you Fred. I'll go and tell Philip what we've discovered so far. With a bit of luck, he might also have heard how his former colleagues at the Yard are getting on with the investigation.'

Augusta climbed the staircase to the mezzanine floor and went through the door which opened into Philip's rooms. His office was a little further down the corridor and the door was closed.

Augusta was just about to knock when she heard voices from within. Philip was speaking to a woman, and she sounded like Mrs Dashwood.

Augusta turned to go back to her shop. And as she did so, the two voices rang out in laughter.

What could they possibly have found so funny?

Augusta didn't like to picture Philip in his office laughing with Mrs Dashwood. And how could the woman do such a thing while her husband remained missing?

Augusta returned to her shop, annoyed at herself for feeling envious.

Chapter 16

PHILIP CAME DOWNSTAIRS to see Augusta later that day. 'It's been a busy day,' he said. 'Time for a break.'

'Is there still no sign of Mr Dashwood?' asked Augusta.

'No. As each day passes, I fear it's going to be an unfortunate outcome. Mrs Dashwood is very upset.'

'Did she visit you earlier today?'

'She did.'

'I thought I heard her laughing.'

'Laughing?'

'Yes. I was about to knock on your door when I heard you had someone in your office with you. So I turned away, and that's when I heard you both laughing.'

Philip pulled a puzzled expression. 'Laughing isn't a crime, Augusta.'

'No, of course it's not. It's just that when you describe Mrs Dashwood as upset… it was just a surprise, that's all.'

Philip said nothing, but gave her a curious glance. As the moment began to feel uncomfortable, she regretted bringing the topic up.

'I suppose our conversation was a little light-hearted at

one point,' he said. 'I told her a funny story about something Herbert, my dachshund, did once. It's important to keep spirits up with a funny story now and again.'

'I see.'

'If I didn't know you better, Augusta, I would say that was an expression of disapproval on your face.'

'No, not disapproval,' said Augusta, 'I was just a little surprised by the laughter. But now that you've explained it, it makes sense.'

'Good. I have to help my clients feel at ease. They need to know that I'm here to help them.'

'Excellent. That seems like the right approach.'

'Wonderful.'

They held each other's gaze for a moment, then Philip scratched at his chin. 'For a moment, I've forgotten what I was going to tell you, Augusta. Ah, that's it! I've remembered now. Here's something you'll be interested in. I had a drink last night with an old friend who works in K Division. His name's Inspector Mansfield and he's based at Deptford police station. I asked him what he knew about the Stevenson's factory there and he told me something quite interesting.'

'Really?' Augusta felt relieved they had returned to normal, easy conversation now.

'Apparently a lady called in at the station a few weeks ago to report an attack on her daughter,' said Philip. 'She said her daughter had been attacked in revenge for speaking to a news reporter about conditions at the factory.'

'That's awful,' said Augusta. 'Was the reporter Miss Foster?'

'She didn't know the name of the reporter.'

'Were the attackers caught?'

'No. Apparently the young woman was followed home

from the factory by two men. Inspector Mansfield has had no luck finding them yet. He suspects they were hired to carry out the task.'

'Dreadful. Was the young woman seriously injured?'

'A broken arm, and cuts and bruises apparently. The shock of the incident is likely to have upset her a great deal.'

'It will have. So James Stevenson ordered the attack on her?'

'We don't know.'

'But he must have done! This demonstrates what an unpleasant man he is. If he's willing to hire two men to attack a young woman who works for him, then I should think it's likely he could have ordered the murder of Miss Foster. Has your colleague informed the Yard about this?'

'Not yet, but I've asked him to. I know that if I were working on this case, I would interview James Stevenson and see what the man has to say for himself. I can only hope my former colleagues will do the same. You do realise who's in charge of the case though, don't you, Augusta?'

'It's the Commissioner's son, is it?'

'I'm afraid so. Detective Sergeant Joyce.'

Augusta groaned. Joyce had recently worked with Philip on the murder case in Westminster. Then Philip had been moved off the case so Joyce could manage it. He was one reason Philip had left Scotland Yard, he had been angered by the move. Joyce was only in his position because of his family connections. He didn't have enough experience to do the job he had been given.

'I can't imagine them making much progress with him in charge,' said Augusta. 'Can't they put someone with more experience on it?'

'He'll be working with a team of colleagues,' said Philip. 'And they'll probably do a lot of the work for him. It

EMILY ORGAN

doesn't seem right, but maybe Joyce has to fail at something before his father realises how hopeless he is.'

'But that means the case is compromised. It's not fair that it shouldn't be investigated properly just because the Commissioner insists on putting someone incompetent in charge.'

'I agree, Augusta, it's not fair at all. But no one's going to march into the Commissioner's office and tell him that, are they?'

'The Yard will lose more good detectives if it's not careful,' said Augusta. 'Anyway, it is what it is. It would be useful to speak to the mother of the woman who was attacked and find out more about the circumstances. It's so frustrating that we can't do it.'

Philip took a piece of folded paper from his pocket and handed it to her. 'I'm not quite sure how this came to be left on the bar after I spoke with my old friend, Mansfield. I'm sure he doesn't know how it got there, either. As far as you're concerned, Augusta, you also found it lying about somewhere. It might be an idea to destroy it once you've read it.' A customer entered the shop. 'I'll leave you to get on with it.' He smiled and headed for the staircase.

Augusta opened the slip of paper. On it was written a name and an address in Deptford.

Chapter 17

JAMES STEVENSON WAS STILL in bed when the police called on him.

'Tell them to come back later,' he said to his butler as he pulled the bedclothes over his head.

'They're from Scotland Yard, sir. I don't think they'll take kindly to such a request.'

James groaned and pulled away the bedclothes. 'Then they're going to have to wait for me to dress then, aren't they?'

'I shall inform them you will join them shortly, sir. It's not advisable to keep Scotland Yard detectives waiting too long. You don't want them thinking you're trying to avoid them.'

'I'm not trying to avoid them, Barnes. I was asleep!'

'Presumably they made an assumption you would be up and about at half-past ten in the morning, sir.'

'Well more fool them. Can you make me some coffee, Barnes? I need to wake up.'

. . .

TWENTY MINUTES LATER, James sat in the drawing room with the detectives from Scotland Yard. For some strange reason, the more senior of the two was the younger one. He had fair, side-parted hair and a boyish face. A sparse moustache ran along his top lip. His name was Detective Sergeant Joyce. His companion was a gruff detective constable who said little but wrote a lot in his notebook.

James felt relieved that he didn't find the pair intimidating. The sooner he could pretend to cooperate then get them out of his house, the better.

'We're investigating the murder of a young woman,' said the detective sergeant. 'Her body was found in a rowing boat floating adrift on the Thames three days ago.'

'I've read all about it in the papers,' said James. 'Awful! But I can't think for one moment why you're here asking me about it.'

'Do you know the identity of the woman?'

'I heard she was a news reporter or something. That's all I know.'

'That's right. Miss Ellen Foster, a reporter for the *London Weekly Chronicle*. Do you read the *Weekly Chronicle*, sir?'

'No. I take *The Times*. I don't really read that either. I just skim through it while I'm eating my boiled egg at breakfast. Now, can you tell me why you're here?'

'If you were a regular reader of the *Weekly Chronicle*, sir, then you would be aware of an investigation the newspaper was carrying out into working conditions at your factory in Deptford.'

'Oh that. I remember hearing something about it. I pay little attention to such things. You must speak to my advisor, Mr Grimston. He handles these matters.'

'I shall make sure I speak with him. But it's also important that I speak with you, too, Mr Stevenson. Can I ask if you read any of the articles in the *Weekly Chronicle* about your factory?'

James shook his head. He couldn't be bothered with this so soon after waking up. 'Mr Grimston showed me some of them, but I took little interest in them. Like I say, Mr Grimston is the one you need to speak to. I believe he took it up with the newspaper editor.'

'Another young woman, Miss Kitty Beaumont, was attacked in Deptford a week ago.'

James lit a cigarette to mask his irritation. 'And what does that have to do with me?'

'Did you hear about the attack?'

'No. I don't live in Deptford. I live here in Mayfair.'

'But you have a factory there.'

'So that means I attacked a woman there? What nonsense this is. You're wasting my time here. I don't have to answer these pointless questions.'

James could feel his temper getting the better of him. He inhaled on his cigarette and tried to calm down.

'Miss Beaumont was a worker at your factory,' said Detective Sergeant Joyce. 'She was too scared to report the attack to us, but her mother did. Apparently, she was attacked because she'd been talking to a news reporter. The young woman was clearly a source of information for the news reporter's articles about your factory in the *London Weekly Chronicle*. It seems someone at your factory found out and a punishment was meted out to her.'

'What? I don't know anything about this!' He stared at the pair of them, mouth agape.

'But it's your factory, sir.'

'A factory which is managed by my advisor, Mr Grimston. I feel very sorry for the woman who was attacked, although she shouldn't have been talking to a news reporter about my factory.'

'So you acknowledge that someone at your factory ordered the attack on Miss Beaumont? Perhaps to make an example of her and deter others from speaking out?'

'No, I don't acknowledge that at all. I'm just surprised to hear about all this. There must have been some misunderstanding. All I know is a newspaper printed a lot of rubbish about my factory. Rubbish which it presumably learned from a woman who worked for me and was unhappy in her job. Who isn't unhappy in their job? Employees in all my factories are regularly complaining about their pay, their hours, and their responsibilities. They seem to expect a decent wage for practically nothing in return! It's sheer laziness and nothing more. And when they feel like they're getting nowhere with their demands, they decide to speak to a news reporter who believes every word they say and puts it into print. I can't believe newspaper editors are complicit in such things. It's slander and defamation, that's what it is! I believe Mr Grimston is looking into legal action as we speak.'

'So you deny knowing anything about the attacks on Miss Beaumont and Miss Foster?'

'Absolutely.'

'Even though both of them have a connection to your Deptford factory.'

'It may be my factory, Detective, but I really know nothing more than I've just told you. I didn't realise Miss Beaumont had been attacked. And I also don't see what my factory has to do with the death of the reporter, Miss Foster. I realise she was reporting what Miss Beaumont had told her, but she would have been working on similar stories too. She was clearly going about writing so much rubbish about everyone that someone got fed up with her and put a stop to it.'

'And would you have any idea who that person could be?'

'None! I have no idea at all! I'm sorry to have completely wasted your time, Detective. But I'm even more sorry that I was woken up early and dragged out of bed for a completely pointless conversation.'

Chapter 18

AUGUSTA MADE her way along Watergate Street in Deptford, looking for number twenty-three. The houses were old and terraced, and their doors opened directly onto the street. A group of grubby faced children played outside a shabby timber-clad shop selling general wares.

The door of number twenty-three was opened by a gaunt-faced woman who was probably in her forties but looked older. She wore an apron over a worn-looking blouse and skirt, and her hair was scraped back from her face.

'Yes?' she said.

'I'm sorry to disturb you,' Augusta said. 'But I'm a private investigator, and I'm investigating the murder of a news reporter, Miss Foster, who I believe spoke to a woman called Kitty Beaumont. Does Miss Beaumont live here?'

The woman folded her arms and gave Augusta a stern look. 'And what do you want to speak to her about? She's gone through enough trouble as it is. It was because of that news reporter that she was attacked on her way back from the factory. She doesn't want to speak to no one about it.'

'But would you mind asking Miss Beaumont? I'm interested in the murder because I actually discovered the news reporter in the boat.'

The woman raised her eyebrows. 'That can't have been a nice find.'

'No, it wasn't. It was quite upsetting. And I think it's awful that Miss Beaumont and the reporter have both been attacked. We need to find out who's behind it.'

'That's what the police are supposed to be doing. Not that they seem to be doing much about it at the moment. Kitty didn't even want the attack reported, she was that scared. I told the police, but they've done nothing as usual. No one's going to get arrested. It's always the same, isn't it? The powerful people always get away with it.'

'Kitty is your daughter?'

'That's right. My name's Mrs Beaumont.'

'And you think someone powerful was behind the attack on your daughter?'

'They had to be. It must have been the factory. They found out she'd talked to a reporter and they attacked her, then dismissed her from the factory.'

'She was dismissed?'

'Yes, she was. There was no need for them to do either of those things. Just a word with her would have been enough. It just shows they've got something to hide.'

'I agree,' said Augusta. 'I'd like to find out what they're hiding.'

Mrs Beaumont thought for a moment. 'I'll ask Kitty if she wants to see you. But don't take it the wrong way if she doesn't. She's been very upset by all of this.'

Augusta waited on the doorstep as Mrs Beaumont spoke to her daughter. She returned a moment later.

'Well, she's alright with it. But she's wary, so be careful

what you ask her.' She moved to one side. 'You'd better come in.'

Augusta thanked her and stepped into the house.

Kitty Beaumont sat on a threadbare armchair in a room which served as both a kitchen and a living room. A little window looked out over a dismal back yard. Kitty's left arm was in a sling.

'I'm sorry to hear what happened to you,' said Augusta.

'I'm trying to forget about it.'

'I'm not surprised. And I'm sorry that no one has been arrested yet for the attack.'

'No one ever will be.'

'I hope they will. Like you, I'm rather frustrated with the pace of the police investigation. I suspect the attacks on you and Miss Foster are linked. We need to find out who carried them out. You didn't deserve what happened to you, and Miss Foster didn't deserve to lose her life.'

'She did!' Kitty's vehement response surprised Augusta. 'She promised she wouldn't tell anyone she'd spoken to me, but she went back on it! They attacked me for it!'

'Are you sure she told someone?' asked Augusta. 'It's very unusual for a news reporter to reveal their source.'

'How else would they know who I was? If she hadn't told them, then I would have been left alone.'

'Do you know for certain that it was Miss Foster who revealed your identity?'

'It had to have been her.'

'Maybe it was someone else who saw you together.'

'Like who?'

'Someone from the factory, perhaps. Where did you meet with her?'

'A few places. Tea shops and the park.'

'So those were public places where you could have been seen together.'

'I suppose so. But I never saw no one I knew from the factory when we met. If someone saw us, then they must have seen us from a distance. That's why I'm sure it was her who said something. I can't think who else could have reported me.'

'I can understand why you think it was Miss Foster,' said Augusta. 'But she had no reason to tell anyone who she was speaking to at the factory. It wouldn't have helped her at all. It's difficult because she's not here to explain herself. But at the moment, I would like to believe that Ellen did everything she could to protect your identity.'

'Maybe she wrote Kitty's name down in her notebook,' said Mrs Beaumont. 'And someone found it.'

'That's a possibility,' said Augusta. 'Obviously, the management of the factory would have been concerned as soon as the first article about working conditions was published in the *London Weekly Chronicle*. Once that happened, they were probably keeping an eye on all their staff to discover who'd spoken to the news reporter. And who knows, they may even have been watching Miss Foster herself, just to see who she was speaking to.'

'Following her around, you mean?' asked Kitty.

'It's possible. It's the sort of thing a desperate factory owner might do.'

'It makes sense,' said Mrs Beaumont. 'Maybe we shouldn't be blaming the reporter after all.'

'All the same,' said Kitty. 'I wish I'd never done it. I wish I'd never spoken to her. I just wanted something to be done about the accident. My friend, Milly, had to have her arm amputated after it got trapped in the power press machine. It was horrible! And they pretended like it never happened! They said it was all her fault when it wasn't.

The machine should have had a safety guard on it. The accident never got reported, and they gave her money and told her to leave. It was a lot of money too. Three months' wages. They said she had to tell everyone the accident was her fault. How can she find work again when she's missing an arm?'

'It sounds like the factory is badly run,' said Augusta. 'Did you speak to your supervisor about it?'

'Yes, but he didn't listen. I wrote a letter to Mr Stevenson, but I don't know if he even read it. Mum helped me write it, didn't you, Mum?'

Mrs Beaumont nodded. 'I think Mr Stevenson just ignored it.'

'What was Ellen Foster like?' asked Augusta.

'She was nice. And she was interested in what I had to say. She was trying to help.'

'How did you meet her?'

'Outside the factory. I saw Miss Foster waiting by the gates for a few days in a row. She was trying to speak to people about the factory, but they didn't want nothing to do with her. Now I can understand why! It was soon after Milly's accident and I'd received no reply to my letter, so I decided to speak to her. Miss Foster was surprised that some accidents weren't being reported as they should. I told her I didn't feel safe with the machines and she seemed very interested in that.'

'How many times did you meet with Miss Foster?'

'About four or five times. I told her that the managers didn't care about the workers. She told me she was doing some research about the factory and had found there were a lot of problems there. I thought that if the newspaper wrote about it then the problems would be sorted out. I hoped Miss Foster would help. But look what happened to her. And I got attacked too.'

'You were lucky you weren't murdered like she was, Kitty,' said Mrs Beaumont.

Kitty nodded. 'It turned out that talking to Miss Foster made everything worse.'

Augusta was just about to ask another question when a woman stepped into the room. She was broad shouldered with a mean-looking face and narrow eyes.

'Martha,' said Mrs Beaumont uneasily. 'Not now.'

Martha was glaring at Augusta.

'Who's this?' she said. 'And what does she want?'

Chapter 19

'THIS IS MRS PEEL,' said Mrs Beaumont. 'She's a private investigator and wants to talk to us about Kitty's attack and the murder of the reporter, Miss Foster.'

'It was all her fault Kitty was attacked!' said Martha. 'She deserved it.'

'Martha is my eldest daughter,' Mrs Beaumont explained to Augusta 'She was very upset about what happened to Kitty. She's protective of her.'

'Mrs Peel says it might not be Miss Foster's fault,' Kitty said to her sister. 'Someone from the factory might have seen me talking to her.'

Martha sneered at Augusta. 'Why are you defending her?'

'I can't be sure exactly what happened,' said Augusta. She noticed Martha's fists clench and tried to choose her words carefully. 'But I know it's unusual for a news reporter to tell anyone who their source of information is. Perhaps Miss Foster did tell someone, but I don't know why she'd do such a thing. I think it's more likely the reporter was followed by someone from the factory and they saw her with Kitty. That's just a guess of mine, though.'

'You don't know, do you? Until someone can prove to me that reporter didn't give Kitty's name away, then I'm going to believe she did. I'm not saying she did it on purpose, it might have been by accident. But it was enough for them to attack Kitty. I blame Miss Foster for what happened. She shouldn't have spoken to Kitty in the first place. She should have just spoken to the managers about it.'

'But the reporter wouldn't have got a straight story from the managers, would she, Martha?' said Mrs Beaumont. 'Miss Foster could see Kitty was a nice young woman who was happy to talk about it sensibly. The managers wouldn't have told her anything. They're just trying to protect themselves.'

'She put Kitty in danger!' said Martha. 'And she didn't care about it. All she wanted was information from Kitty. But look what happened to her. That could have been Kitty too. We're lucky she's still here.'

'Miss Foster can't defend herself now, Martha,' said Mrs Beaumont. 'I don't think we should keep blaming her when there are other explanations. I think someone from the factory could have been following her.'

'Mrs Peel's convinced you now, hasn't she Mum?' said Martha. 'But she won't convince me. I know what she did. She was playing with danger and that's why she's dead. That's what happens when you don't care about others. Now Kitty can't work because they dismissed her from the factory and she's got a broken arm. There's no justice. The only justice is that Miss Foster is dead now.'

'Martha!' said her mother. 'That's no way to speak about someone who's passed away!'

Martha shrugged and gave Augusta another hard stare.

Chapter 20

AUGUSTA FELT pleased to return to her shop, away from the intimidating gaze of Martha Beaumont. Why had she been so unfriendly? Was she hiding something?

Fred had placed a pile of *Aristo* magazines on the counter. 'These are all the copies I could find which had James Stevenson or the Crawford sisters in,' he said.

'Thank you, Fred! I hope this is going to help us.' Augusta picked up a copy with a photograph of a doe-eyed society beauty on the cover. '"Miss Lillian Fraser-Macintosh,"' she read out from the caption. '"Daughter of Captain Fraser-Macintosh and engaged to Sir William Thornton-Hildyard." Well, I wish the happy couple well, don't you, Fred?'

'I do indeed. Now, I've marked each relevant page with a bookmark. Not actually a bookmark, but a strip of newspaper. My mother wouldn't let me turn down the page corners. She likes to re-read these.'

'Very well, I'll treat them carefully.'

Augusta turned to the bookmarked page and peered at a set of photographs which showed groups of smiling young people in expensive clothes and jewellery and holding glasses of champagne.

A tall, slim, fair-haired lady in a shimmering dress caught Augusta's eye. She looked like a mannequin in a shop window. 'So that's what Rita Crawford looks like,' she said, once she had determined her identity from the caption.

'Yes,' said Fred. 'Bridget looks similar, she's slightly shorter and has darker hair. They're the sisters who go to all the parties. Apparently, they once spent a night in Madame Tussauds as a dare. They disguised themselves as waxworks and weren't discovered until the morning.'

'How lovely to have the time and energy to do such things.'

'Indeed,' said Fred. 'If they had to earn an honest living like the rest of us, they'd be tucked up in bed by ten o'clock every night.'

'Is that the time you go to bed, Fred?'

'Yes. Every night.'

'I suppose I'm a bit of a night owl. I struggle to get to sleep much before midnight.'

'I can imagine that, Augusta. The trouble with you is that your mind never switches itself off, does it?'

'It certainly doesn't.' Augusta turned back to the pile of magazines. Now let's see what James Stevenson looks like. Eventually she found him in a photograph taken at the birthday party of a West End actress. He looked about thirty-five and had regular features, but his wide, fleshy mouth gave him a toad-like appearance. He was smartly dressed and Augusta could see he might be considered handsome. But once she had the idea of a toad in her mind, she didn't find him attractive at all. 'He doesn't look like a factory owner, does he?' she said to Fred.

'No. He looks like someone who would rather do

anything other than manage factories. I suppose he inherited them, and so he's stuck with them.'

'Poor chap,' said Augusta with a smile. 'Do you think we should feel sorry for him?'

'From what I hear of him and what I see in the photographs, I struggle to like him,' said Fred. 'But he doesn't look the sort to murder someone, does he? I realise this might sound silly, but there's something rather innocent about his face. He merely looks like a young man who has inherited a lot of money and likes to spend his time socialising.'

'It says here they're in The 99 Club.'

'They're always in The 99 Club, according to *Aristo*.'

'Is that so?' Augusta could feel an idea developing. 'I'm going to see if Philip is free to talk.'

Chapter 21

'YOU'VE PUT UP A SHELF,' said Augusta, as she stepped into Philip's office. It was a little shelf which occupied the middle of the large blank wall opposite Philip's desk.

'It looks good, doesn't it?' He grinned. 'Actually, you've reminded me to put something on it.' Philip got to his feet, picked up his book of Sherlock Holmes stories, walked across the room, and placed it on the shelf. 'It has to lie down for now,' he said. 'I need two bookends.'

'And a few more books.'

'Yes, a few more books would be nice. Fortunately, I know a good place near here which sells those. What's the name of the shop again? Oh, that's right. *Webster's.*'

'Watch out,' said Augusta. 'Don't forget the landlord here is a friend of Lady Hereford's. I can request your removal if you upset me.'

'You wouldn't dare.' Philip made his way back to his desk. 'Anyway, it's nice of you to visit me up here, Augusta. Have you got something on your mind or are you just being friendly?'

'I've got something on my mind.' She took a seat across

the desk from Philip. 'I've got a plan for how I can bump into James Stevenson.'

'How?'

'Apparently he's always at The 99 Club.'

'That's one of those nightclubs in Soho, isn't it?'

'Yes. And I plan to go there. Why are you smiling?'

'Because it's not the sort of place I picture you in, Augusta.'

'Don't forget the reason we became reacquainted was because I was caught up in that incident at Flo's Club. It's not unheard of for me to attend these places, you know.'

'I realise that, but you visited Flo's Club as a chaperone, didn't you? To go there as a reveller is a little different.'

Augusta laughed. 'I'm not exactly a reveller!'

'That's my point.'

'But I can set foot in these places for a drink.'

'Are you going to go on your own?'

'I think I'll have to. Who else could I ask to go with me? Fred tells me he's in bed by ten o'clock every evening. Places like The 99 Club don't get going until after then. I should be alright on my own. I won't need to stay there long.'

'Or you could ask me to go with you.' Augusta laughed. 'What's so funny?' asked Philip.

'You can't imagine me in a place like that, and I can't imagine you there either. We'll both be mistaken for someone's parents.'

Philip chuckled. 'We probably will. Does that matter, though? We could pretend we're there to fetch home our wayward daughter who's stayed out after her curfew.'

'Well, that's settled then. How about this evening?'

'Yes, why not? The sooner the better.'

'We can do our best to mingle with the crowd, even

though they'll all be about twenty years younger than us. By the way, I visited the Beaumont family this morning.'

'You've been to Deptford and back already? I'm impressed.'

'It's quite clear the Beaumont family blames the reporter, Miss Foster, for the attack on Kitty Beaumont. I explained to them it's unlikely Miss Foster told anyone the name of her source. I suggested someone from the factory may have been following Miss Foster and discovered Kitty's identity that way.'

'A good possibility. And what did they make of that suggestion?'

'I think Kitty and her mother were willing to consider the idea.'

'I think it's the most likely explanation,' said Philip. 'As soon as the management at the factory knew someone was talking to the *London Weekly Chronicle*, then they could have arranged for the reporter to be followed. I agree with you, Augusta, news reporters are careful with confidential information. I have experience of trying to get certain information from them and they guard their sources carefully.'

'Despite what I told the Beaumonts, there's a member of the family who wasn't convinced and continues to blame Miss Foster. Her name is Martha, and she's Kitty's older sister. To be honest with you, Philip, I don't have a good feeling about her. I found her aggressive and confrontational. And she was clearly furious about the attack on her younger sister.'

'Understandably so. But there's no evidence that Miss Foster gave Kitty's name to anyone, and there are other plausible explanations for how Kitty came to be identified as the informant.'

'Is there any possibility of finding out whether Martha Beaumont has been in trouble with the police in the past?'

'There could be something in the records at Deptford police station. Why do you ask?'

'Because there was something scary about her. She looks like the sort who'll happily use her fists if she needs to. If she's prone to violent outbursts, then who knows what she's capable of?'

'You think Martha Beaumont could be a suspect in the murder of Miss Foster?'

'I think it's worth investigating her. Kitty was attacked a week before Ellen Foster was murdered. It's a possibility she was murdered in revenge for the attack on Kitty.'

'By Martha Beaumont?'

'Possibly.'

'I'll have a chat with Inspector Mansfield in Deptford. If I can persuade him, he might have a look in the records for us. I hope he's also making progress with catching the men who carried out that attack on Kitty. But even if Martha Beaumont does have a violent history of causing trouble, it doesn't mean she's responsible for Miss Foster's death.'

'I realise that. But we've been assuming the Stevenson family could be behind it. It's important to realise there are other suspects too. And Martha seems just the sort of person who might lose her temper and do something awful.'

'You're usually a good judge of character, Augusta.'

'But perhaps I am being a little judgmental? And maybe I met her at a bad moment. She certainly didn't like me being in her home, and I can understand that. But if she does have a record of being violent in the past, it would be worth trying to establish an alibi for her at the time of Miss Foster's death, wouldn't it?'

'Absolutely, Augusta. I'll speak to Mansfield and see

what he says. Officially, however, we're not working on this case, are we?'

'No.'

'So we have to be careful. If the Yard finds out we're speaking to people about it, then we could be in trouble.'

Chapter 22

'I'VE JUST ENDURED a visit from Scotland Yard,' said James Stevenson as he sat in the high-backed leather armchair in Grimston's Pall Mall office. 'It should have been you answering their questions, not me!'

'Believe me, sir, if I had known that detectives from Scotland Yard would be calling on you, I would have made arrangements to attend.'

'They don't give anyone any notice, do they? They do it on purpose so they can catch you unawares.'

'I suspect they do.'

'But even so, I don't expect to have to sit in my own home and try to answer to your actions!'

'Which actions are those, sir?'

'The attack on one of the workers. Apparently she was punished for speaking to the press about working conditions at the Deptford factory. Now don't tell me this is something you cooked up, Grimston.'

'I didn't cook up anything, sir. I don't know what you're talking about.'

'Why would two men attack a woman in the street and

warn her not to speak to the press? I can only imagine you discovered it was her who'd been speaking to that murdered reporter.'

Mr Grimston cleared his throat and James felt convinced the old man looked guilty. 'As you know, Mr Stevenson, the reports in the *London Weekly Chronicle* have been most concerning. I entered into many conversations with the editor of the *Weekly Chronicle*, but to no avail. At the same time, I asked some of the supervisors at the factory to make inquiries among the staff to find out who had been speaking to the news reporter. After all, the nonsense clearly began with one of our workers, didn't it? I can only assume the reporter paid good money to hear tall tales about the factory. A young woman by the name of...' He looked through some papers on his desk until he found what he was looking for. 'Miss Beaumont. She was identified as the person who had spoken with the news reporter.'

'What was the evidence?'

'I don't know. I was informed by one of the supervisors that she had been identified. And that's all I know of it.'

'So who attacked her?'

'I have no idea, sir.'

'So when you discovered Miss Beaumont had spoken to the reporter, you did nothing more about it?'

Grimston settled back in his chair. 'I merely trusted the supervisors to deal with it.'

'And that's what they did? They attacked her?'

'I don't know if they were responsible for the attack or not. It would be disappointing if they were. I merely assumed a word would have been had with her about it.'

'A word would have been enough, I think! Attacking her in the street is a bit heavy-handed. And the trouble is this sort of thing comes back to me! Scotland Yard now thinks I had something to do with that attack when I didn't even know anything about it! Why didn't you tell me about it?'

'I knew nothing about it, either. One of the supervisors mentioned she wouldn't be returning to the factory and I asked no more questions.'

'Which supervisor?'

'Mr Granger. But I wouldn't worry about taking it up directly with him, sir. I think the matter has now been dealt with.'

'Except it hasn't. I've got Scotland Yard sniffing around. And because of this attack on Miss Beaumont, they seem to think I'm brazen enough to actually have murdered the reporter too!'

'Now that's just ridiculous, sir.'

'Of course it is! But you try telling that to the police, they won't listen. It's obvious what they're thinking. If we attacked one of our workers, then we probably murdered the reporter too. This doesn't look good for me!'

'I agree, sir, it doesn't. I would like to remind you I warned you about how damaging these news articles would be when they first began appearing in the *Weekly Chronicle*. I informed you that the matter needed to be dealt with as soon as possible.'

'Yes, I remember you saying that. And you were the one who was supposed to be sorting it out.'

'I did what I could, sir. I spoke with the editor of the *Weekly Chronicle*. However, I think it would have been better if you had spoken to him yourself.'

'I leave you to manage my affairs, Grimston. I told you I don't get involved with speaking to editors of newspapers.'

'Well, the situation is as we find it. I feel quite certain it will all blow over. If the police want to make an arrest over the attack on Miss Beaumont, then they can arrest one of the supervisors. You and I were ignorant of what they did.'

'But the detectives were practically accusing me of murder this morning, Grimston! They're not going to leave me alone, I know it. I have a motive for wanting the reporter dead and yet I didn't get involved in any of this business. This is being poorly managed. My father paid you to look after the business, and I pay you to do the same.'

'With all due respect, your father took a little more interest in the business than you, sir.'

'Because he was a businessman! He was a natural at it. Although I realise my responsibilities, I can't manage them on a day-to-day basis. That's why I need your help, Grimston. And when something goes wrong, I don't expect to have to take the blame for it!'

Chapter 23

MR GRIMSTON MADE a telephone call after James Stevenson left his office.

'I thought you might like to know that he's just visited me.'

'And how was he?' asked the voice at the other end of the line.

'Angry. He says the police are blaming him for the attack on Miss Beaumont. He's also worried they think he murdered Miss Foster, too. He's an obvious suspect, of course, but I didn't tell him that.'

'What did you tell him about Miss Beaumont?'

'I told him I had no knowledge of the attack and that it must have been something some supervisors arranged. If need be, we could encourage one or two to resign from their posts just to show we don't tolerate such behaviour at the Deptford factory. That should satisfy him, although there's a risk it will suggest to the police that the factory was behind the attack.'

'It's already obvious.'

'Yes, I suppose it is.'

'Hand a couple of people over to the police, then we can wash our hands of it. But we can't have the police speaking to James without you there.'

'I agree. He doesn't handle these things well and his hot-headedness could land us in even more trouble. I've asked him to telephone me as soon as he hears from them again.'

'Good. And keep me informed, Anthony.'

'I will do.'

Chapter 24

AUGUSTA'S REPAIR of *The Moonstone* was almost complete. She had reattached the covers and fixed the spine. All she needed to do now was refresh the lettering and embellishments on the cover with gold leaf. She slid a thin, delicate, shiny square of the material out of an envelope and was just about to apply it when a knock at the door disturbed her.

'There's a gentleman here to see you, Augusta,' said Fred. 'He says his name is Mr Ferguson.'

The name was familiar, but Augusta couldn't place it for a moment. As she stepped into the shop, she recalled it was the name of the reporter for the *London Weekly Chronicle* who she had met with Titus. And now the man stood in the centre of her shop, his eyes and red moustache twitching with satisfaction that he had surprised her.

'Mr Ferguson,' said Augusta. 'I didn't expect to see you here.'

'I thought you might be surprised,' he said. 'Although I was expecting to be pounced on by that dog of yours when I set foot in here.'

'A friend of mine looks after him when I'm working in the shop.'

'But you have another pet here, I see.' He walked over to Sparky in his cage. 'A budgerigar.'

'A canary.'

'So you're an animal lover, Mrs Peel.'

'Yes, I am. How can I help you, Mr Ferguson?'

'After our encounter the other day, I was interested in finding out a little more about you.' He glanced around. 'This is a delightful shop you have here, Mrs Peel. I'd have visited you sooner if I'd known how good it was.'

Augusta disliked him. He had a smug manner and was refusing to explain the reason for his visit.

'You didn't mention you owned a bookshop when we met on Fleet Street,' he continued.

'No. I didn't think it was relevant to the conversation.'

'You also didn't tell me you used to work for British intelligence.'

A rush of cold ran through her. How had he found this out?

He smiled, clearly enjoying her shocked response. 'I'm an exceptionally good news reporter, Mrs Peel. If I want to find out information, then I can. What I'd like to know is why you were waiting for me outside my office the other day.'

He was an arrogant bully. Augusta decided to show him he didn't intimidate her one bit. And she reasoned there was no use in making up any tales to cover herself. If she was honest with him, it would be difficult for him to find fault with her story.

'I wasn't waiting for you, Mr Ferguson. I didn't know who you were until we spoke. But I'll admit to you that I was waiting outside your offices. I wanted to meet a colleague of Miss Foster's.'

'And why was that?'

'Because I saw the boat she was in adrift on the Thames. I didn't know Miss Foster, but I'm keen to find out what happened to her.'

'You're quite good at these sorts of cases, aren't you, Mrs Peel?'

'You've done some research into my previous cases, I expect.'

'You're right. I have. With Detective Inspector Philip Fisher of Scotland Yard. Although I understand he no longer works for the Yard and is now a private investigator.'

He paced slowly around the shop, gazing at bookshelves and pulling out occasional books as he spoke. She wanted him to leave, she didn't like him being here. Fred was watching him like a hawk, and she could tell from his expression that he didn't warm to the man either.

'You still haven't explained how I can help you, Mr Ferguson,' said Augusta.

'I don't think there is anything you can help me with, Mrs Peel. You paid me a visit, so I'm returning the favour.'

'You happened to be the first person who stepped out of the door of the *London Weekly Chronicle* offices,' said Augusta. 'I didn't purposefully try to meet with you.'

'So what did you want Miss Foster's colleagues to tell you?'

'I wanted to understand more about the circumstances behind Miss Foster's death.'

'Do you suspect her colleagues?'

'How could I possibly do that? I know very little about Miss Foster and her work. Are you suggesting I should suspect one of them?'

'Not at all, Mrs Peel. But as you consider yourself an

amateur detective, I can only assume you suspect everyone at this stage.'

'That's common in an investigation.'

He turned to her and fixed her with his pale green eyes. 'I think you're dead set on solving this one. But it will be difficult for you when you're unable to operate in any official capacity as a detective. And your detective friend is no longer working for the Yard. It leaves the pair of you quite powerless, doesn't it?'

Augusta could feel her teeth clenching. 'Even if that is the case, Mr Ferguson, I don't see what business it is of yours.'

He took a step towards her, and she fought the urge to move away from him. 'And I don't see what business it is of yours that my dear colleague was so brutally murdered. I suggest you leave it to the police to do their job.' He took a step back again and smiled. 'I can see that I've angered you. Now you know what it's like when someone turns up out of the blue and asks you questions. Perhaps we should agree from now on to stay out of each other's way. What do you think?'

Chapter 25

AUGUSTA CALLED in at a dress hire shop before heading home that evening. She hired a midnight blue low-waisted dress which was trimmed with sequins at the hem and neckline. She reasoned it was fashionable enough for The 99 Club, but not too fashionable that she would look foolish in it. The shop assistant also persuaded her to hire a matching headband decorated with fake jewels and a large feather.

When she got back to her flat, she set some rollers in her hair and kept them in while she ate some soup and bread and put on some make up. By the time Philip arrived at eight o'clock, she was ready.

'Good grief, I barely recognised you!' he said as she answered the door.

'Is that good or bad?'

'Well, that's difficult to answer.' He walked into her flat, leaning on his walking stick. 'If I say it's good, then that implies it's a vast improvement on your daily appearance, and I wouldn't want to suggest that. And if it was a bad thing, that would suggest you didn't look good enough for this evening. And I think you look marvellous.'

'Thank you, Philip. I shall take it as a compliment.'

'You should. Absolutely.'

'And you look smart yourself.'

He looked down at his dark suit. 'Thank you. I could have chosen a brighter tie, I think. I'm going to look rather dull standing next to you.'

'Nonsense! How about a quick drink before we hail a taxi?'

'That's an excellent idea.'

Augusta poured out two whiskeys, then told Philip about Walter Ferguson's visit as they sat in her living room.

'How annoying I wasn't there!' said Philip once she had finished.

'I don't think there was a lot you could have done.'

'I would have told him to sling his hook, that's what I would have done! What an unpleasant man walking into your shop and bullying you like that.'

'He didn't succeed in scaring me. If that's what he wanted.'

'Good. And the obvious question is why he wanted to scare you in the first place.'

'Usually when someone turns nasty, it means I've got closer to the truth.'

'Perhaps he murdered his colleague.'

'Perhaps he did,' said Augusta. 'We need to know what his motive could have been.'

'If I were working on this case, then I would interview the editor of the *London Weekly Chronicle* and find out what the relationship was like between Mr Ferguson and Miss Foster,' said Philip. 'But as I'm not involved, I can't do that. I'll check with Joyce though, hopefully he's spoken to the editor. Oh, look at the time. We had better get going.'

. . .

THEY HAILED a taxi on Marchmont Street and arrived at Wardour Street in Soho ten minutes later. They stepped out of the car into crowds of revellers on the pavement.

'Pretty much everyone here is younger than us, Augusta,' said Philip, glancing around. 'But I'm not going to let that put me off. I'm going to pretend that I'm twenty-five again.'

Augusta laughed. 'And I'm going to do the same. And if anybody gives us a funny look, it's their problem rather than ours.'

The entry fee for The 99 Club was a pricey twelve shillings. Once they had paid, they descended a dark, steep staircase down to the basement. The frenetic rhythm of a jazz band grew louder as they went.

'Are you alright on these stairs, Philip?' said Augusta, aware he would find them difficult with his walking stick.

'Of course I'm alright on these stairs! I'm twenty-five, remember?'

'Oh yes. I forgot.'

'How could you forget?'

They entered the dingy fug of the nightclub. A tangle of people whirled on the dance floor while others sat in a semi-circle of candlelit tables.

They found an empty table and ordered drinks from a waiter in a white jacket.

'So this is where all the fashionable people come?' shouted Philip over the noise of the band. 'It seems a little overrated, if you ask me.'

'That's because you're not a bright young thing,' said Augusta with a laugh.

'Excuse me? I like to think I'm a bright thing at the very least!'

Augusta scanned the crowd for James Stevenson. It wasn't easy in the dim light. The couple of drinks had given her a warm, relaxed sensation, and she watched the dancers as her foot tapped to the music.

'I recognise this song,' said Philip. 'The band in that auberge in Roeseloare used to play it. Do you remember?'

'That's where I've heard it before! I knew it sounded familiar.' The recollection brought with it other memories of Belgium and the war which Augusta preferred to forget. They both sat quietly for a moment with their thoughts.

Then Augusta saw a face she recognised.

'That's him!'

'Where?'

'At the bar talking to the man in the pin-striped suit. I'd recognise that toad-like face anywhere.'

'Toad-like?'

'Yes.'

'Ah yes. I see what you mean now. He does resemble a toad, doesn't he? Well, I'm relieved he's here. I was beginning to worry he wasn't going to turn up.'

Augusta adjusted her headband and smoothed her dress. 'I'll go and speak to him.'

'Do you want me to accompany you?'

'He might feel threatened if we both approach him. And besides, you don't want the Yard finding out you've spoken to him.'

'Good point, Augusta. I'll keep my nose clean. I'll wait here and you know where I am if you need me.'

Chapter 26

AUGUSTA TRIED to ignore her nerves as she made her way to James Stevenson at the bar. He wore an expensive suit and his dark, oily hair was slicked back from his face.

As luck would have it, James's companion was distracted by someone else as Augusta drew near.

'I recognise you from *Aristo*,' she said to James.

He gave her a bemused look. 'That's the reason you want to talk to me?'

Augusta was aware she wasn't young and attractive enough to be of much interest to him. She had to say something to keep his attention.

'My name is Augusta Peel and I'm a private investigator. I discovered the body of the news reporter Ellen Foster floating in a rowing boat on the River Thames.'

James Stevenson rolled his eyes. 'I can't get away from it, can I?'

'Only because she wrote some accusatory things about your factory.'

'So everybody thinks I have something to do with her death.'

'Have you got any idea who could have harmed her?'

'None whatsoever. She was a troublemaker, and clearly someone had had enough of her. I can't blame them. But I had nothing to do with it. I've already had the police asking me questions. I don't need you harassing me about it, either.'

'What about the attack on the worker from your factory who was supposedly talking to Miss Foster?'

'I've got nothing more to say to you. If you continue asking me these questions, I'll ask the management to throw you out. And who are you anyway? A private investigator? Working for who? I don't want to discuss any more of this now. I'm here to have fun. Please don't approach me or any of my friends here again.'

AUGUSTA RETURNED TO THE TABLE.

'You don't need to tell me how that went, Augusta,' said Philip. 'Your expression says it all.'

'He was rude and defensive. And showed no concern for either of the women who were attacked. He seems primarily interested in protecting himself.'

'That's interesting.'

Augusta sighed. 'Maybe I approached it the wrong way. I think I was too direct. Perhaps I could have got a better response if I'd prepared myself better.'

'If he's feeling defensive, then no amount of preparation is going to get you anywhere with him.'

'I feel like our evening has been wasted.'

'Why?'

'Because all I managed was a short, rude conversation with him.'

'Isn't that often the way? At least you've learned more about his character. And the fact he showed no concern for the two victims is suspicious. I think most ordinary people would say something sympathetic.'

'He doesn't seem like your average ordinary person.'

'That's because he isn't. He's inherited a fortune and spends much of his time in dingy, noisy places like this. He lives in a different world to the rest of us and maybe he follows different rules too.'

'Which means you can attack and murder people whenever they annoy you?'

'It's possible. Let's get another drink and observe him for a while.'

Augusta gulped the next drink, keen to wash away the disappointment of the bruising encounter with James Stevenson.

'How's Mrs Dashwood?' she asked Philip.

'She's managing alright, but it's been five days now since her husband disappeared. It's frustrating that I can't get to the bottom of it.'

'Do you see her every day?'

'Yes. She doesn't have much family, so she needs someone to support her.'

'I can imagine she finds you very supportive.'

'I like to think so.'

'She's quite attractive.'

'I suppose she is. But why do you mention it, Augusta?'

'Oh I don't know.' The drink had gone to her head and envy about Philip and pretty Mrs Dashwood now took over. Before she could stop herself, Augusta spoke some more. 'Do you think she finds you attractive?'

'What sort of question is that?'

'I think she does.'

'She's a married lady, Augusta!'

'Perhaps she and her husband were having problems?

Perhaps he left her and she doesn't want to admit it? Or perhaps the truth is more sinister.'

'What?' He stared at her with a scowl on his face. 'Sinister? What are you suggesting? She murdered him?'

'She could have done. Have you considered that? Or are you too blinded by her beauty?'

'Good grief, what a load of nonsense.' Philip got to his feet. 'I don't like the change in this evening's mood. I'm going to hail a taxi to take you home, Augusta.'

Chapter 27

IN DEPTFORD, Martha Beaumont walked along Butchers Row. It was a narrow, cobbled street which wound its way around the rear of the riverside warehouses. A solitary streetlamp lit her way.

She clasped the sackcloth bundle in her hand and hoped she wouldn't encounter anyone else at this late hour. She wasn't frightened, she knew how to look after herself. But she didn't want to be answering questions.

At the end of Butchers Row, she turned left into the narrow alleyway which led to the steps down to the river's foreshore. She couldn't see much, but she knew this place well.

The glow of a cigarette end in the darkness made her stop. A dark figure stood at the top of the steps.

Someone was in her way.

'Who's that?' called out a young man's voice.

She recognised it immediately. 'What are you doing here, Billy?'

'Martha? I could ask the same of you.'

She had known Billy since childhood, and he was harmless. The trouble was, she needed him gone.

'How's Kitty?' he asked.

Martha didn't want a conversation. She wanted to get this over and done with.

'She's been better.'

'What's happening with the blokes that did it?'

'We'll get them.'

'Let me know if you need help.'

Martha smiled, knowing Billy couldn't see her face in the darkness. There was no chance of him helping deal with the men who had hurt Kitty. Billy couldn't fight his way out of a paper bag.

The bundle felt weighty in her hand. She needed to get rid of it quickly. If anyone came along and demanded to see what she was holding, then she would be in trouble.

If she asked Billy to move so she could get to the steps, he would ask her what she was doing. There was a risk he would tell someone he saw her go down the steps, too. It was an unusual thing to do at this time of night.

Billy began relating a story about a mutual friend who had lost his job. Martha clenched her teeth. How long was he going to talk for?

She thought about what to do next. Tell Billy to shut up? Threaten him? Maybe she could throw a punch which would knock him out cold so she could get on with what she needed to do.

As he continued to talk, she switched the bundle to her left hand and clenched her right fist.

Poor Billy. He wouldn't hurt a fly. But he was in the wrong place at the wrong time.

As he laughed at a point in his story, she took a step closer to him. His silhouette was clear now against the night sky and the lights of the north riverbank.

A surge of anger seethed in her chest. She just needed him to be quiet.

Her body tensed and Billy seemed to sense something was wrong. He stopped talking and the glowing cigarette end dropped to the ground where it was extinguished with a grind of his boot.

'I'm going to catch last orders at the Mason's Arms,' he said. 'You coming?'

Martha's shoulders relaxed, and she released the grip in her right hand.

'No, I'm going for a walk. I'll see you around, Billy.'

He went on his way and she waited for his footsteps to die away before she headed for the stairs.

The wooden steps were steep and slippery. Martha descended as carefully as possible. In front of her, the wide dark river slipped by silently.

The foreshore was muddy and littered with rocks, stones and debris. The dank smell of the river filled Martha's nostrils. It was a smell she had known all her life. Everyone in her family had been born within three hundred yards of this spot.

She tripped on the uneven ground a few times before she felt sure she was close enough to the river. Then she stretched her arm back with the bundle in her hand before launching it as far as she could in a slingshot movement. She heard the bundle land in the water with a satisfying splash.

The job was done.

Chapter 28

AUGUSTA FELT awful the following morning. Her head ached, and she felt tired and nauseous. Worst of all, she was filled with regret after accusing Philip of being blinded by Mrs Dashwood's beauty.

She tried to distract herself by feeding seeds to Sparky. But the memory of her drunken outburst replayed in her mind. It made her grimace and cringe. She wished there was something she could do to change what had happened. But she was powerless to do anything about it. She had upset Philip and revealed herself to be an unreasonable, jealous person.

'Did you have a nice evening, Augusta?' asked Fred.

'It was alright. I spoke to James Stevenson. It was easy to recognise him thanks to your copies of *Aristo*.'

'You spoke to him?'

'Yes, but he didn't appreciate it. He was quite rude, in fact.'

A customer interrupted them. She was a short, wide, bespectacled lady in a grey woollen overcoat. She paid no attention to the books on the shelves and instead walked up to the counter and stared at Augusta through her thick-lensed spectacles.

'Can I help you?' Augusta felt a little disconcerted.

'Are you Mrs Peel?'

'Yes, that's right.'

'I've just been reading all about you.'

Augusta felt a lurch in her unsettled stomach. 'Reading about me? Where?'

'In the *London Weekly Chronicle*.' The woman pulled a folded-up newspaper out of her handbag and placed it on the counter. 'There's an article here all about you.'

Augusta's heart sank. 'What does it say?'

The lady unfolded her newspaper. '"Secret life of London bookseller",' she said. 'That's what the headline says. Then it says here that you own a bookshop but you're also a private detective.'

'I'm not officially a private detective. I've just helped with some cases.'

'It says here you were a private detective and that you used to work for British intelligence during the war.'

Augusta sighed. This was the work of Walter Ferguson. 'Nobody interviewed me for the article, so I can only imagine most of it is incorrect.'

'Is it? Well, it's an interesting read, anyway. I thought I'd come and see what you were like.'

'And do I meet your expectations?'

The lady's eyes narrowed behind her thick lenses. 'Not really. I thought you'd be taller.'

Augusta heard Fred snigger. 'Perhaps you'd be interested in the books I sell here,' said Augusta.

'I'm not much of a reader myself.'

'I see. The only reading material you like is the *Weekly Chronicle*, is it?'

'Yes, I get it every week. I live quite close by so I thought I'd come and have a look at you.'

'Well, you've had a look at me now. And, as you're not here to buy anything, perhaps you'll be content to go on your way?'

'Yes, I probably will.'

The woman snatched the newspaper from the counter and Augusta watched her leave.

'I wanted to ask her if I could read that article, but it would have made her stay in this shop longer,' she said to Fred. 'What a strange woman. I'd better go out and buy myself a copy.'

AFTER A VISIT TO A NEARBY NEWSAGENT, Augusta stood at the counter and read the article which Walter Ferguson had written about her. He described her as a bookseller masquerading as a private detective. Philip was described as a close friend who had recently left Scotland Yard under a cloud. He had found out little about her work in Belgium during the war, but Augusta was annoyed he had mentioned it at all. It was work which had been necessary at the time but best forgotten about now. It wasn't the sort of thing she wanted people to know she had done.

Philip would want to see the article because he had been mentioned in it. Reluctantly, Augusta made her way to his office and prepared to see him for the first time since the embarrassment of the previous evening.

Chapter 29

WALTER FERGUSON BOUGHT a copy of the *London Weekly Chronicle* outside Camden Town tube station so he could read it on his journey into work. On the tube, he made himself comfortable and turned to pages five and six for the article on Augusta Peel. He sipped from his hip flask as he read his work. The editor had made some minor alterations, but it had come out well.

Walter smiled to himself as he thought about Augusta Peel's reaction when she read the article. He knew it would annoy her, that's why he had written it. It served her right for ambushing him outside the office. She was one of those dangerous people who thought she was cleverer than she actually was. From what he could see, she wasn't a remarkable investigator at all. She had solved a few crimes, but she had been helped by Detective Inspector Philip Fisher. If she had solved them by herself, he would have given her more credit.

He had done quite a lot of research on Augusta, but he hadn't yet found out how she had been chosen to join British intelligence during the war. He could only imagine that she had known someone who had asked her to help with the war effort.

She had worked closely with Mr Fisher during the war. He had assisted her then, just as he assisted her now. She was probably reliant on him. And perhaps Mr Fisher was reliant on her? It was an interesting relationship between the pair of them. And he had also discovered that Mr Fisher's wife had left him at the end of the previous year. Had that been something to do with his friendship with Mrs Peel? Or had that been something else?

Augusta was a secretive woman who had revealed little about herself. Most mysterious of all was her time before the war. He knew she was forty-one years old. That meant she had already been in her mid-thirties when the war had broken out. What had she been doing before then?

There was another mystery too. Her name, Mrs Peel, suggested she was a married woman. And yet Walter couldn't find any evidence of a Mr Peel, nor any record of a marriage. He couldn't find anyone who remembered Mr Peel or recalled Augusta mentioning him.

What was she hiding? He planned to answer this question for his second article about her.

Chapter 30

'GOOD MORNING,' said Augusta meekly as she stepped into Philip's office.

'Good morning Augusta!' His cheery manner surprised her. She had expected him to be sulky with her. 'How are you feeling?'

'Horrible.' She sat in the chair opposite him. 'I'm so sorry for my outburst last night. It was completely uncalled for and unreasonable and I'm thoroughly embarrassed I behaved in that way.'

'Please don't worry about it, Augusta. You were disappointed about getting nowhere with James Stevenson and you'd had a few drinks.'

'That's no excuse.'

'Yes it is. Just use it as an excuse, Augusta. Please don't feel bad about it. We all get moments where we…'

'Embarrass ourselves?'

'Exactly.'

'My comments about Mrs Dashwood were extremely unreasonable. Especially when she's going through such a difficult time. I don't think she murdered her husband.'

A smile played on Philip's lips. 'That was some accusation.'

'It was a silly suggestion. Anyway, I'd like to try and forget about it now.' She handed him the copy of the *London Weekly Chronicle*. 'You need to turn to pages five and six.'

She watched Philip as he read through the article, tutting and shaking his head at moments.

'Well you really have annoyed Walter Ferguson, haven't you Augusta?'

'I suppose this is some sort of intimidation tactic. Presumably he wants me to know that he can find out whatever he wants about me.'

'The mention of British Intelligence is completely uncalled for. It wouldn't surprise me if the *Weekly Chronicle* finds itself in trouble with the War Office over it. In fact ,I think I shall alert the War Office to this article. These events shouldn't be discussed, and identifying the names of those who worked in intelligence is out of order. Walter's clearly the sort of man who bears a grudge, but what about the editor? He shouldn't have allowed this to be published. What a lapse in judgement.'

'I get the impression Walter Ferguson is keen to prove he's an accomplished investigator,' said Augusta.

'Well, if he's that good, you'd think he would be investigating the death of his colleague, wouldn't you?'

'If he or someone else at the newspaper was behind it, then that would explain his lack of interest.'

'Exactly. At times like this I wish I was still employed by the Yard. I would haul him in for a long, arduous interview.' He folded up the newspaper and threw it into his wastepaper bin. 'You didn't want to read any more of it, did you Augusta?''

'No.'

'Good. I've heard back from my friend Inspector Mansfield in Deptford. I asked him to look up Martha Beaumont's history and he obliged. It turns out you were correct, Augusta.'

'About what?'

'Martha Beaumont has a violent past. She's been arrested three times for violent conduct. On each occasion, she was inebriated, and it was late in the evening after pub closing time. She's clearly the sort of woman who likes to throw her weight around.'

'So she can be aggressive.'

'It seems so. But as you know, there's quite a difference between being drunk and violent in the street and using a gun to carry out a well-planned murder.'

'Does she have an alibi for the time Miss Foster was killed?'

'I don't know. But I've suggested to Mansfield that he telephones young Detective Sergeant Joyce at the Yard and tells him about it. Hopefully the pair of them can investigate Martha further.'

A knock at the door interrupted them.

'Come in!' said Philip.

Mrs Dashwood stepped into the room. She wore a laurel green coat over a stylish carnation pink dress. An expensive-looking handbag was looped over one arm and she held a pair of silk gloves in one hand. Her outfit was fresh and springlike, and a posy of forget-me-nots was tucked into the band of her hat.

'Oh, I'm sorry, I didn't realise you had company, Philip!'

'It's only Augusta. Come and take a seat. How are you, Laura?'

It hadn't escaped Augusta's notice that they addressed each other by their first names.

'As well as can be. Six days it is now!' She rested an elegant hand on her chest. 'I don't know how I'm holding up. Actually, I do know.' She turned to Augusta. 'Philip is helping me enormously, Mrs Peel. This has been the worst time of my life and I haven't known what to do with myself. My daily routine has just stopped. Everything is on hold. I'm just waiting and waiting until I hear news of Leonard. I can't imagine when I'll see him again. It might be tomorrow. It might be next week. It might be next month. It might be... I can't bear to think about it. And I can't tell you how helpful Philip is. I don't know what I'd do without him. He puts my mind at ease. Not completely at ease, of course, because it's awful not knowing what's happened to your husband. I keep hoping that one day I'll wake from this awful dream, and he'll be here. But Philip's always here and it's such a consolation to me. There's something about his manner, isn't there? He's very calm and everything he says makes so much sense. He doesn't come out with silly platitudes just to make me feel better. He genuinely makes me feel better about everything.'

'How lovely to hear it,' said Augusta, forcing a smile. 'I'd better get back to my shop.'

Chapter 31

'HOW DID you feel when you heard your sister, Kitty, had been attacked?'

Martha Beaumont folded her arms and glared at the young detective who had asked her the question. Was he the best Scotland Yard had? He didn't look much older than her and was fair-haired, with a scrappy moustache. He had told her his name was Detective Sergeant Joyce. He was accompanied by Inspector Mansfield, who she had met before at Deptford police station. Mansfield was older and had a steel grey moustache with no hint of scrappiness about it at all. They sat in a spartan interview room at Deptford police station.

'Obviously, I was upset when my sister was attacked,' said Martha.

'Did you understand why she was attacked?' asked Joyce.

'Something to do with that news reporter.'

'Did you know your sister had been talking to Miss Foster, the news reporter?'

'Yes, she mentioned it. It was a stupid idea.'

'Did you tell her that?'

'No, she doesn't listen to me.'

'Would you not have done the same if you had been in your sister's situation?'

'Spoken to a news reporter? No.'

'Why not?'

'No point.'

'And why do you say that?'

'Because it changes nothing, does it? Look where it's got Kitty. Nowhere. She's got a broken arm and no job. And the news reporter's dead. It's more trouble than it's worth. You don't want to take on these people, they're too powerful.'

'Which people?'

'You know the people I mean. And you know who harmed Kitty and you can't get them. They're too powerful. They're the people who own factories. Rich people. You can't say stuff about them because they come after you. So you have to keep quiet about it.'

'Except you're not the sort of young lady who keeps quiet about things, are you?' said Inspector Mansfield.

She sneered at him. He couldn't resist bringing up her past misdemeanours.

He looked down at the papers in front of him. 'We've arrested you three times, haven't we, Miss Beaumont? For drunkenness and violence.'

She shrugged. 'Don't see what that's got to do with anything.'

'What I mean by it is that you're not the sort of young woman who sits back and does nothing, are you? If need be, you will defend someone you care about.'

'Of course I would. And so would anyone. You would as well, Inspector.'

'But we're not talking about me, are we? We're talking

about the fact you must have been very upset when your sister was attacked.'

'I was. I've already said that. But if she hadn't talked to the reporter, then she wouldn't have been attacked.'

'You believe in using your fists rather than talking, is that right?'

'Sometimes I use my fists, sometimes I talk. Depends on the situation.'

'And you've used your fists to resolve disagreements, haven't you, Miss Beaumont?'

'Yes. Sometimes I have to. Especially if something's happened to my friends or family.'

'But you used more than your fists when you encountered Miss Foster, didn't you?'

'I never met her!'

'What were you doing on the evening of the first of May?'

'I was in the pub.'

'Which one?'

'The Mason's Arms. Where else? And you can ask everyone who was in there, and they'll be able to tell you that.'

'What time did you leave the pub?'

'Can't remember.'

'And where did you go after you left the pub that night?'

'Home.'

'You live with your mother and sisters, is that right?'

'Yes. You can ask them what time I got back because I can't remember.'

'Did you go anywhere else between leaving the pub and returning home that evening?'

'No.'

'Perhaps you did, but you don't remember?'

She gave a snort. 'What's that supposed to mean? How can I tell you if I don't remember it?'

It was true she had gone somewhere else that evening, but she wasn't going to admit it to them. They could question her all day and all night and she wouldn't confess to anything. As far as she was concerned, she went to the pub, then she went home. She felt sure her mother and sisters wouldn't remember the exact time she had returned.

'Is it possible that you encountered the news reporter, Miss Ellen Foster, on the evening of the first of May?'

'No. Like I told you, I never met her. You're trying to make me say I murdered Miss Foster in revenge for what happened to Kitty? But that's not true. And where would I have got a gun from?'

'You know a few criminal types around here, Miss Beaumont. If you really wanted to get your hands on a gun, I think you could manage it.'

'Maybe. But that doesn't mean I shot the news reporter, does it? And besides, you'd never find me anywhere near a boat. I don't like water and I can't swim. You're wasting your time asking me these questions. When are you going to catch the men who attacked my sister? If you'd caught them sooner, none of this would have happened!'

Chapter 32

'THE COPS THINK I murdered that stupid news reporter,' Martha said to Kitty when she returned home. Kitty was sitting on the front doorstep trying to darn a sock with one arm in a sling.

'She wasn't stupid. She was nice!'

Martha shook her head. Kitty always wanted to see the best in people. She was too trusting. 'She got you into trouble.'

'You heard Mrs Peel say she wouldn't have given my name to anyone. Someone must have followed us.'

'Do you know that for sure?'

'I didn't notice anyone following us. But they would have hidden, wouldn't they? They would have followed us in secret. Ellen Foster didn't deserve what happened to her. And I know there's no chance you would have murdered her! Why do they even suspect you?'

'Because Inspector Mansfield knows what I'm like. And he thinks I wanted revenge after what happened to you.'

Martha sat down on the step next to Kitty and sighed. 'I wish you'd never spoken to her.'

'So do I! I only did it because of what happened to Milly. And there were the other accidents too. I didn't feel safe, and Ellen was the only person who listened to me.'

'But she couldn't do anything about it, could she? All she did was write about it in the newspaper and that caused even more trouble! Look what happened to her. You should never have bothered with it.'

'I know.' Kitty turned to her, her brow creased with worry. 'Are they going to arrest you, Martha?'

'I don't know.'

'I'll go down to the station and tell them you didn't do it! I know you could never do a thing like that. I know you were angry when I got attacked, but you would never have taken revenge like that. I can tell the police that. I'll tell them I know you better than anyone!'

Martha smiled and put her arm around Kitty's shoulders. Poor Kitty. She didn't know her big sister at all. But she was extremely caring and loyal. Too trusting.

'Thank you, Kitty, but you don't need to speak to them. I can look after myself.'

'But how?'

'I'll come up with a plan. If they think it was me, then they'll have to prove it. And they can't prove anything right now.'

'So what will you do?'

'I'll think of something.' She gave Kitty's shoulder a squeeze. 'I always do.'

Chapter 33

'I FINALLY FINISHED REPAIRING *THE MOONSTONE*,' said Augusta, showing the book to Fred.

'It looks like new! It's such a lovely edition too. I hope you're going to give it a decent price.'

'I think six shillings should do it.'

'Six shillings? But you've spent ages repairing it. I think you could price it at ten.'

'That's too much.'

'No, it's not. Not for this edition. In fact, I think you often under-price your books, Augusta.'

'Really?'

'Yes. I popped into a second-hand bookshop on Charing Cross Road at the weekend. Just to be nosy. Their books are much more expensive than ours.'

'And I bet customers take one look at them and go elsewhere.'

'No, I saw people buying books.'

'But it's Charing Cross Road. It's famous for its bookshops.'

'I think you should price *The Moonstone* at ten shillings,

Augusta. And if no one buys it, and you're keen to sell it then you can reduce it. But if someone does buy it, then you've made ten shillings!'

'Alright then, you've persuaded me.' Augusta picked up a pencil, opened the book and wrote ten shillings on the fly cover. 'Let's see what happens.'

She heard footsteps on the mezzanine floor above their heads, then Philip descended halfway down the stairs and gave her a wave.

'Would you mind joining us for a moment, Augusta? I have an interesting visitor.'

'Mrs Dashwood?'

'No!'

'Who is it then?'

'Come and see.' He grinned.

'Fine,' said Augusta. 'But I'm quite busy at the moment.' She walked over to the stairs.

'Aren't we all?' Philip began to climb the stairs back to the mezzanine floor. 'But I think you're going to be quite amused by this.'

Augusta followed Philip to his office.

A young man was sitting in the chair at Philip's desk. He got to his feet as they entered the room. He had fair, side-parted hair and a sparse moustache.

'Detective Sergeant Joyce,' said Augusta. 'This is a surprise.'

'Mrs Peel.' He politely bowed his head, and she took the seat next to him.

'The three of us haven't been together since that murder case in Westminster Abbey,' said Philip as he made himself comfortable behind his desk. 'Perhaps you can tell Mrs Peel what you've just told me, Joyce?'

'Yes. Indeed.' The young man cleared his throat. 'I'm here because we need your help.'

Chapter 34

'OUR HELP?' said Augusta. 'With which case?' She thought it would be fun to pretend she had taken no interest in what had been going on.

'The tragic murder of the news reporter, Miss Foster,' said Joyce. 'I understand you noticed the boat she was found in, Mrs Peel?'

Augusta nodded.

'The case is proving quite tricky,' continued Joyce. 'And I must say that your presence, Mr Fisher, is much missed at Scotland Yard.'

Philip said nothing. The commissioner hadn't hesitated in replacing Philip with his son, and Philip no doubt considered it was the fault of the Yard that they were now missing his expertise.

'The obvious suspect is James Stevenson. I hear you spoke to him at The 99 Club, Mrs Peel?'

'That's right. Yesterday evening.'

'I paid him a visit this morning, and he was most annoyed by it. He complained that he's being harassed by the police and that a lady detective accosted him during his evening out.'

'I happened to see him there,' said Augusta. 'And I thought it would be interesting to find out what he had to say about the murder of the news reporter. I asked him a couple of questions and he was grumpy with me, so I left him alone. If you ask me, he's a man who's got something to hide.'

'What makes you say that?'

'When you speak to someone about a murder, they're usually appalled. But James Stevenson showed no sympathy for Miss Foster at all. Nor any sympathy for Miss Beaumont who was attacked because she spoke to Miss Foster. He didn't appear to care about either of them.'

'Is that so? That's quite telling.'

'It is. Either he's the sort of man who never cares about anyone else, or he's hiding something.'

'Or it could be both,' said Philip.

'I have to say that I haven't got much from him either,' said Joyce. 'And he has a miserable companion called Anthony Grimston who has managed the Stevenson family business for many years. Trying to get anything out of him is like trying to get blood from a stone.'

'Who else have you spoken to about the murder?' asked Augusta.

'Mr Baker, the editor of the *London Weekly Chronicle*, has been quite helpful.'

'What did he have to say for himself?'

'He's extremely upset about the death of Miss Foster. He told me she was his most valued reporter. He was very fond of her.'

'Fond of her?' said Philip. 'That sounds intriguing. Fond in a romantic way, would you say?'

'Possibly,' said Joyce. 'Although I'm certain it wasn't reciprocated.'

'Did Mr Baker tell you anything about Miss Foster's relationship with her colleagues?' asked Augusta.

'Not much. But I did have a chat with a pretty secretary there and she told me there was some resentment because Miss Foster was a favourite of Mr Baker's.'

'Interesting,' said Philip.

'Have you spoken to Walter Ferguson?' asked Augusta.

'Who's he?'

'A strange man who was a colleague of Miss Foster's. He's a news reporter at the *Weekly Chronicle*. In my conversations with him, I've not noticed him express any sadness about Miss Foster's death. In fact, he's just the sort of character who would have been resentful of Mr Baker's favouritism of her. He's so odd that he's written an article about me in this week's edition.'

'Why has he written an article about you?'

'I happened to bump into him and ask him some questions about Ellen Foster. He didn't like it, so he appears to have written an article about me out of vindictiveness. He's an unusual character. I think you could do with interviewing him.'

Joyce took his notebook from his pocket and wrote down Walter Ferguson's name.

'Then there's Martha Beaumont to consider,' said Augusta.

'Ah yes, the sister of the young woman who was attacked. I spoke to her this morning. Inspector Mansfield at Deptford station thinks she could have murdered Miss Foster in revenge for the attack on her sister.'

'How did the interview go?' asked Philip.

'She was quite confrontational. There's no doubt she's a fearless young woman. And she has a reputation for violence too. Inspector Mansfield is quite familiar with her.'

'James Stevenson, Walter Ferguson and Martha Beaumont,' said Philip. 'Three very different characters who all had a motive for murdering Miss Foster. What can you tell us about the victim, Joyce?'

Chapter 35

'AS YOU KNOW, Ellen Foster's body was discovered in a rowing boat which was found floating adrift on the Thames on the morning of the second of May,' said Detective Sergeant Joyce. 'The police surgeon believes she was shot the previous night. So when she was discovered, we think she had been dead for ten to twelve hours. That means time of death was likely to have been between ten o'clock and midnight. There were two gunshot wounds and a bullet was retrieved from the body, it was lodged against the collarbone.' Augusta winced. 'We think the gun was a Webley revolver. The weapon hasn't been found. And despite their detailed knowledge of the river, the river police can't tell us where the boat entered the water.'

'Really?' said Philip.

'The tides make it difficult to ascertain.'

'I see.'

'The last time Miss Foster was seen alive was when she left the *London Weekly Chronicle* offices on the day she died,' said Joyce. 'The editor, Mr Baker, says she left at six o'clock that evening. We can't find any further sightings of her after that time.'

'Where did Miss Foster live?'

'She rented a room at a house in Clerkenwell. We've spoken to the landlady, Mrs Collins, and searched the room for clues. But we didn't find much.'

'What sort of things were you looking for?' asked Philip.

'Diaries, letters… any other personal papers which might have given us some clues.'

'And you couldn't find any?'

'No. There was very little in her room.'

'How strange. Is it possible someone could have gone into her room after her death?'

'It's possible, but they'd have to have a key. Her landlady obviously has a key, and she hasn't seen anyone go in or out of the room.'

'Any sign of forced entry?'

'None. But perhaps Miss Foster wasn't the sort of lady who kept personal records and papers.'

'It's possible,' said Philip. 'But unlikely, I'd say. Many people keep a diary, and just about everyone has a stash of letters and correspondence somewhere. I'd like to speak with the landlady. What do you think, Augusta?'

She nodded. 'Good idea.'

'Well, let me know how you get on,' said Joyce. 'It's important we keep each other informed.'

'Of course,' said Philip. 'And hopefully we can get this one solved.'

'There's a lot to do,' said Joyce. 'I've told my father I need some assistance with this case. The Yard is quite stretched at the moment, we've got a lot of cases on the go. My father has agreed to pay for the services of a private detective to assist us.'

'I'm not after any money,' said Augusta.

'I am,' said Philip. 'How much is he offering?'

'I'll have to ask him.'

'If the offer's good enough, then I'll consider helping,' said Philip.

Augusta smiled. She knew that whatever the offer was, Philip was desperate to work on the case.

'WELL DONE on securing Scotland Yard as a client,' Augusta said to Philip once Detective Sergeant Joyce had left.

He rubbed his hands together with glee. 'It's not a bad move, is it? Not only can we work on the case, but we get paid for it too. I shall make sure you receive your fair share, Augusta.'

'I've told you before, I own a bookshop. I'm not officially a private detective at all. I refuse to take money for it. The reward I get is seeing justice done.'

'Oh, how I wish I could be as principled as you, Augusta. I jumped at the first opportunity to be paid for the work.'

'That's because you have this new business. You need to earn money.'

'You're right, Augusta. I do. But this is a wonderful development, isn't it? I know Detective Sergeant Joyce is a bit wet behind the ears and rather hopeless at his job. However, if we work with him, we can find out everything that's going on in the investigation. And we have the freedom to do our own work on it too. I'm going to enjoy this.'

'Make sure you don't forget about Mr Dashwood.'

'No, I shall make sure of that, Augusta. But to be honest with you, I'm not holding out much hope for him.

He's been missing for six days now. It's quite mystifying. I'm beginning to think he made the decision just to take off. Perhaps he was unhappy in his marriage and didn't know how to explain it to his wife. Maybe he's walked out and is making a new life for himself somewhere.'

'That's what you're going to say to Mrs Dashwood?'

'No, I can't possibly say that to her. Can you imagine how upset she would be? But I've done what I can to find him. I've spoken to his friends and family and colleagues, and to be honest, there aren't many of them. He seems to have kept himself to himself most of the time. I put an appeal for witnesses in the newspaper, for people who may have been on the same tube train as him that evening. But nothing. I've also repeatedly checked with the local hospitals to see if there are any patients matching his description. And nothing again. It's very frustrating. And the sad reality is that some people just simply go missing and are never found again.'

'I find that very hard to understand. I realise the world is a big place, but surely someone must know something when someone is missing?'

'I agree, Augusta. And perhaps one day we'll find out. If he hasn't gone off of his own accord, then all it takes, I suppose, is a fall into some deep water. There are plenty of canals in London and let's not forget the river too. Perhaps one day his remains may be uncovered. But I don't want to say that to Mrs Dashwood either, do I? She'd be dreadfully upset. I'll continue to work on the case, but there's only so much I can do.'

Chapter 36

ELLEN FOSTER HAD RENTED a room in a house in Northampton Square in Clerkenwell. A light drizzle fell as Augusta and Philip tried to locate the address.

The square had probably been a smart address in Regency times, but now it was occupied by tradespeople such as printers, jewellers and furriers. There were a few scruffy lodging houses too, including the one where Miss Foster had lived.

'Not more detectives,' said Miss Foster's former landlady at her front door. She was a tired-looking lady in her fifties with a large bosom and short wavy hair. Her eyebrows had been drawn in with dark pencil and her lips were stained dark pink.

'Ellen Foster lost her life in tragic circumstances, Mrs Collins,' said Philip. 'And until we can find the culprit, we have to keep looking for clues. When did you last see her?'

She sighed. 'I've gone through all this before. It was when she left for work that morning, the day she died. She left here at eight o'clock.'

'Did she mention she was meeting anyone after work?'

'She didn't tell me that directly, but she said there was no need to make any tea for her because she would be back late.'

'But she gave you no further clue about what she had planned?'

'No.'

'Was that unusual?'

'No, it was quite normal. She didn't tell me much about herself. She was a private person. Quiet. She kept herself to herself. She was always very polite and respectful, but she never let on very much. She wasn't much of a talker. Not to me anyway.'

'Did she seem concerned about anything when you saw her that morning?'

'No, not concerned at all. She wasn't the sort of lady who would show her feelings very much, but she just seemed completely normal.'

'Did she have any family that you know of?'

'A sister. She lives a few minutes from here. She has a baby. Her husband died of an illness.'

'That's sad to hear. Do you know the sister's name and address?'

'Yes, Polly. I forget her surname now. She's at number eighteen, Rawstorne Street.' Philip made a note of this. 'Thank you, we'll call on her next. What about friends of Miss Foster's?'

'I think she was too busy for friends. Always working.'

'Did any friends ever visit?'

'No, never. But she only had a small room here, not enough space for visitors. I think she probably met friends in cafes and parks and things, but I wouldn't know about that. She never mentioned no one.'

'Any gentleman friends?'

'I think there was one, but she was secretive about it. She

never actually told me about him, but sometimes I would see a gentleman waiting out here in the square.' She pointed to the gardens in the centre of the square. 'She would go out and meet him there. He never called at the door.'

'Have you any idea who he is?'

The landlady shook her head. 'None. I couldn't even tell you his name. And I didn't like to ask her because, like I say, she was private about these things. I don't think she would have told me much even if I had asked.'

'Can you describe him to us?'

'I'd say he was in his thirties and looked quite respectable. Hat and long overcoat. He looked like he worked in the newspapers like she did. Quite a handsome chap, I suppose. That was all I knew of him. I couldn't tell you anything else.'

'Do you think she met him regularly?'

'I suppose she must have done.'

'Did he wait outside regularly?'

'Not too often. I probably saw him four or five times, maybe six at the most. It's difficult to be completely certain. I didn't exactly keep a record.'

'That's understandable. When was the first time you saw him?'

'I really couldn't tell you.'

'But it was recently?'

'Oh yes, quite recently. The beginning of this year. I didn't see him last year at all. So if it was a romance, then it probably only began this year.'

'Do you mind if we have a look in Miss Foster's room?'

'No. I don't like going in there much myself, but I'll come up the stairs with you and wait outside.'

Augusta was pleased to get out of the drizzle as they followed the landlady into the house and up a winding, creaky staircase to the third floor. She unlocked the door of Miss Foster's room. 'There you are,' she said. 'I'll wait here.'

It was a small, tidy room with a window that overlooked the square. The air had the aroma of a room which had been closed up and unused. A bed, a dressing table and a wardrobe took up most of the space. The dressing table had a couple of drawers which Philip opened. 'Just some writing paper, pens and a hairbrush,' he said. 'Remarkably little as Joyce said.' He raised his voice for the landlady who was standing outside the room. 'My colleagues told me they were surprised by the lack of personal papers in this room, Mrs Collins,'

She poked her head around the door. 'Yes, they mentioned that. They asked me if it was possible she could have put her letters or diaries somewhere else in the house, and I told them no. Everything in that room is as she left it.'

'Is it possible someone visited this room after her death?'

'I don't see how. The door was locked.'

'What happened to her key?'

The housekeeper shrugged. 'I've no idea. She would have had it with her when she was attacked. I suppose the police must have it somewhere.'

'Interesting,' said Augusta. 'So the key has never been returned to you?'

'No.'

'Is it possible the murderer took the key and visited this room?' asked Philip.

'I never saw anyone visit the room.'

'Are you here all the time, Mrs Collins?'

'No, not all the time. I go out from time to time to run

errands. But I'm quite sure no one would have come in and visited her room.'

'But there's a possibility, though,' said Augusta.

'Not really.'

'Just a slight possibility?'

'I doubt very much the killer took her key and visited her room,' said the landlady.

'Would you be willing to gamble ten pounds on it?' asked Philip.

'I'm not a gambling woman! And if I was, no I wouldn't bet ten pounds on it because I suppose there's a chance someone did come here without me knowing.'

'Thank you, Mrs Collins. That's very helpful.'

PHILIP AND AUGUSTA left the house and made their way to Rawstorne Street. 'We need to track down the mysterious gentleman Miss Foster was meeting,' said Philip. 'He's clearly got something to hide, hasn't he? If he was completely innocent of any wrongdoing, then he would have come forward as soon as the police put out an appeal for information. It's quite telling that he's remained silent on the matter.'

'We've got to find him first,' said Augusta. 'We don't have much to go on.'

'No, we don't. Perhaps the sister, Polly, knows something? It will be interesting to see what she can tell us.'

Chapter 37

RAWSTORNE STREET WAS a narrow thoroughfare lined with old, terraced houses which had seen better days. Ellen Foster's sister, Polly, lived on the ground floor of a property opposite a pub.

To Augusta's surprise, Polly didn't hesitate to invite them in. The room was furnished with cheap modern furniture and a baby slept in a pram in the corner.

Polly made them tea in a kitchenette which adjoined the room. She looked similar to her sister, dark-haired with the same thin mouth. She wore a cotton dress with a fashionable sailor collar and bow.

'We apologise for bothering you at a time like this,' said Augusta once they were all sitting comfortably with a cup of tea. 'But we're hoping we can learn a little more about your Ellen so we can find out who is behind her murder.'

'James Stevenson,' said Polly.

Augusta startled at the directness of her reply. 'What makes you so sure it's him?'

'It has to be. She was reporting on the accidents at his

factory and he didn't like it. It has to be him. I've told the police this, but they haven't arrested him yet.'

'They'll be looking for evidence, though,' said Philip. 'And if you're right, then I'm sure they'll find it.'

'I know I'm right.'

Philip opened his notebook and made some notes. 'Do you mind telling me your surname?'

'Hastings. But please call me Polly.'

'What can you tell us about Ellen?' Augusta asked.

'She was quiet and caring,' said Polly. 'We got on well, even though we were very different. I was more interested in becoming a wife and a mother. I never wanted to be a professional lady like my sister. She had always wanted to be a writer or a reporter, so she was doing exactly what she wanted. I feel very proud of her. It wasn't easy for her working for a newspaper, there aren't many lady news reporters about. But she worked hard, and she was clever. She deserved to do well at her job. And she looked after me and William, too.' She glanced at the pram. 'Now that she's gone, he's all I have left.'

'How old is your son?' Augusta asked.

'Nearly four months old.'

'He seems very peaceful.'

'He is at the moment. But he's not always like this.'

'I can imagine.' Augusta smiled.

'My husband died six months ago.'

'I'm so sorry to hear it. It must be a struggle for you.'

Polly nodded. The young woman clearly couldn't work, and Augusta wondered how she managed financially.

'I can imagine Ellen helped you after your husband's death.'

Polly nodded. 'She did. She visited every day after William was born. It wasn't easy for her because she was busy with her job, too. But she always came here after work when he was a young baby, and she visited every weekend. More recently, she left me to get on with things. But that's because I feel I'm able to cope better now. And she still visited at the weekend. She always looked out for me. She was five years older and was always very protective. I remember her standing up for me when we were at school and some girls were mean to me in the playground.' She paused to sip her tea. 'Our mother died when we were young, so our father brought us up. He died a few years ago.'

Tears pricked the back of Augusta's eyes. Polly seemed so lonely.

'Did Ellen ever mention she was seeing someone?' asked Philip.

'She mentioned there was a gentleman, but she said it wasn't serious. I think she worried it wasn't a respectable arrangement. Women are expected to choose either spinsterhood or marriage, aren't they? Courting men here and there is looked down upon. She never wanted to marry because she didn't want to give up her work.'

'Do you know his name?'

'No. And I never met him. I can't imagine it would have been serious between them. I think he was someone she just enjoyed spending time with.'

'Did your sister seem to be worried about anything before she died?' asked Philip.

'No, I don't think anything worried her too much.'

'Was she worried about James Stevenson seeking revenge for the articles she wrote about the accidents at his factory?'

'No, that never worried her at all. She underestimated him.'

'Have you ever met him?'

'No. I've had nothing to do with him. Neither did Ellen. But when she heard about the factory accidents, she quite rightly wrote about them. It's very unfair that he makes his staff work in those conditions. It's dangerous! Have you read the reports Ellen wrote? So many accidents, and he just pretended nothing was happening. That was quite typical of him.'

'Why do you say it was quite typical of him?' Philip asked.

'Because he's obviously that sort of person. He was born into a rich family and didn't have to worry about anything when he was growing up. He inherited all that money and he can do what he wants. He doesn't know what it's like to actually work in a factory. He's never worked a day in his life. Although I'm sure he claims to work hard when he manages his factories.'

Augusta asked, 'Did Ellen discuss her work with you?'

'Yes, she did. I always read everything she wrote, often before she submitted it to her editor. She was a talented writer and a good investigator. I enjoyed reading everything she wrote. And I believe James Stevenson wanted her dead. He needs to be arrested! I don't understand why he's walking about as a free man.'

AFTER LEAVING MRS HASTINGS, Augusta and Philip walked to the tram stop near Sadler's Wells Theatre.

'What did you make of Polly?' Philip asked.

'I feel sorry for her,' said Augusta. 'She's lost her parents, husband and sister.'

'Very difficult. She's putting on a brave face, I think. It was nice to hear more about Ellen because we hadn't known much about her until now.'

'It was. But I feel there's still more to know,' said Augusta. 'Who was the man she was seeing? And why did she keep him secret?'

Chapter 38

'SPARKY, I've just had the most astonishing thought!' Augusta dropped the poetry book she had been browsing onto her lap. 'What if Leonard Dashwood is the murderer?'

Sparky eyed her from the lampshade of the lamp on the side table. He was permitted to roam freely around Augusta's flat each evening before his bedtime.

'When did Mr Dashwood go missing?' continued Augusta. 'I think it was the first of May. And Ellen Foster was murdered late in the evening on the first or in the early hours of the second of May. And Mr Dashwood hasn't been seen since. He could be a fugitive! And this could also explain why Ellen Foster was secretive about her gentleman friend, it's because he's married!'

She paused for a moment and took in a breath. Could she really be right?

'I wonder how Ellen Foster and Leonard Dashwood met. Just a moment... didn't Mrs Dashwood say her husband travelled by tube to and from Charing Cross every day? His workplace must be near Charing Cross.

And that's at the end of the Strand which turns into Fleet Street once you get past Temple Bar. Or where Temple Bar used to stand, they removed the archway when they widened the road. So Fleet Street is only about a mile from Charing Cross tube station. And maybe Mr Dashwood works on The Strand or Fleet Street? He could have encountered Miss Foster somewhere there. Perhaps the two had an affair and she threatened to tell his wife? He could have silenced her. It's a horrible thought, but it's happened before.'

There was a knock at the door.

Augusta got up and looked through the spyhole. 'Philip?'

She opened the door.

'Sorry for calling on you at this late hour.' He walked into her flat, leaning on his stick.

'Is everything alright?'

'Yes. In fact, I have good news. Mr Dashwood has been found!'

'Really? What a funny coincidence, I've just been thinking about him.'

'Why?'

'I'll explain in a moment.' She gestured to the sofa. 'But first, tell me where you found him.'

'I didn't find him,' said Philip, settling into the sofa. 'The fire brigade did.'

'Goodness! How?'

'The fire brigade was called to South Kentish Town tube station this afternoon,' said Philip. 'It's on the Hampstead tube, between Camden Town and Kentish Town. I don't know if you remember, but it closed last year.'

'I do remember. And there was a fire there?'

Philip nodded. 'A tube driver spotted it as his train passed through. Smoke was also seen coming from beneath the door of the shuttered-up ticket office on the street. By the time the fire brigade got there, the fire had quite a hold. It took them a couple of hours to extinguish it and then they searched for its cause. They discovered it had started deep down at platform level and the smoke had travelled up the empty lift shafts to the street. They had to unblock the staircase to get down there. And when they reached the platforms, they discovered a rather distressed Mr Dashwood.'

'Mr Dashwood was on the platform of the tube station? But it's closed! How did he get there?'

'It's on the route he uses to and from work every day. Apparently, on the day he went missing, he was absorbed in his evening newspaper on the tube journey home. The train had to make an unscheduled stop at the closed tube station and the guard mistakenly pressed the button to open all the doors on the train instead of just his own. Mr Dashwood, still absorbed in his newspaper, absentmindedly stepped off the train as he did every day. He normally got off at the next stop, Kentish Town. But he got off at the stop before without giving it much thought.'

'But how? The station must have been in complete darkness!'

'It was. Apparently, he thought there was a power cut in the station. But he only thought that for a moment before he realised his mistake. Just as he turned to get back on the train, the guard closed the doors and off it went.'

'So the guard didn't notice he'd got off?'

'No.'

'And what about the other passengers?'

'I don't know. I suspect many of them were equally engrossed in their newspapers and didn't notice. Perhaps others assumed he was just changing carriages. Anyway, the tube went off and he was stuck in South Kentish Town station. He tried to flag down the next tube train, but the driver didn't see him. Then he tried the next one and so on. But none of them noticed him. He had a box of matches with him and he used some matches to light his way to the spiral staircase. He climbed all the way up it, I think it's about three hundred steps or so.'

'And he discovered it had been blocked off?'

'Exactly. He tried banging at the top of the staircase, desperately trying to get someone's attention from the street outside the ticket office. But no one heard a thing.'

'So that's where he's been all this time? Stranded in South Kentish Town tube station?'

'Apparently so. And all he had with him was a cheese sandwich left over from his lunch and a flask of tea. Every day he hoped someone would spot him.'

'He probably hoped another train would stop there like his did.'

'He reached complete desperation by this morning.'

'I'm not surprised.'

'He managed to make the flask of tea last a few days and he also found a leak where water was dripping down a wall. He was able to collect it in the cup from his flask.'

'Yuck.'

'Indeed. I don't know where that water was leaking from. But without it, he may have died. He was weak with hunger and feared for his life. By this morning, he only had a few matches left, so he bravely used them to make a fire.'

'With what?'

'Advertisement posters which he'd ripped down from the walls.'

'That was smart thinking.'

'It was. If only he had thought of it sooner. He's being treated in the Royal Free Hospital for dehydration and smoke inhalation.'

'Oh goodness. He's lucky to be alive.'

'He is.'

'Well done on completing your first case, Philip.'

'Well done? I didn't do anything!'

'Yes, you did. You did all you could to find Mr Dashwood. You inquired at the hospitals, police stations, printed posters, put notices in the newspapers. You did everything you could.'

'And where did it get me? Nowhere.'

'You weren't to know he was trapped in a disused tube station.'

'No. I don't think I would ever have found him there. But when he lit the fire, that's when he was discovered. Mrs Dashwood is insisting on paying me for my work, even though I did nothing to find her husband.'

'But you still deserve to be paid for it,' said Augusta. 'You spent a lot of time on it.'

'Yes, I did. Although I feel a bit of a failure.'

'You're being much too hard on yourself! You can't expect to solve every single case you work on. And no amount of detective skill would have found him at that deserted train station.'

'But perhaps I could have identified it as a location to search. I knew the route he travelled by each day. I should have remembered the tube station closed recently.'

'Even if you'd discovered that, you would never have expected that the doors had opened at the stop and Mr Dashwood had stepped out. I think Mrs Dashwood was absolutely right to pay you for your work.'

'Well, thank you for helping me to feel a little bit better about it, Augusta.'

'Mrs Dashwood must be overjoyed.'

'She's absolutely over the moon. She told me it's been the worst week of her life.'

'And it's not been a great week for Mr Dashwood, either.'

'It hasn't. Why were you thinking about him earlier?'

'I had a sudden idea. But it's going to sound very silly now.'

'Tell me.'

'Very well. I thought Mr Dashwood might have murdered Miss Foster because he went missing shortly before her death. And I wondered if they had an affair and she was secretive about it because he was married.'

'And you think he murdered her to hide the affair?'

'Yes. But now I've learned he's been stuck in South Kentish Town tube station for six days, it's impossible.'

'You do a good job of considering absolutely everyone as a suspect, Augusta.'

'It's not very charitable of me, is it?'

'No. But maybe that's what makes you a good detective.'

Chapter 39

'HERE'S THE BOAT,' said Inspector Tingle of the Thames River Police the following morning. Augusta and Philip stood with him in a high-walled yard at Thames Police Station on the Wapping riverside.

The last time Augusta had seen this small rowing boat, it had been floating on the river. She pictured again the sight of Ellen Foster's dark hair beneath the tarpaulin. The memory made her chest feel heavy.

'Is there any chance of tracing its owner?' asked Philip.

'No chance.' The inspector gave it a kick with the toe of his boot. 'I'm astonished it stayed afloat, to be honest with you. It looks half-rotten, doesn't it? It's not been maintained. It had probably been abandoned somewhere. Someone probably tied it to a mooring, then forgot all about it.'

'Any fingerprints on it?'

'A few partial prints on the seat, but they're poor quality. As for the rest of the boat, forget about it. You can't retrieve fingerprints from old wood like that.'

'So you think the murderer found this boat and took it?' asked Augusta.

'I suspect so. If someone had owned this, they would have maintained it.' He gave the boat another kick. 'Look how easy that's just splintered there.' He stooped down to peer at the damage.

'So can you work out when this boat was put into the river on the night of the first of May?' asked Philip.

'No.' Inspector Tingle straightened up again.

'No?'

'I've already explained this to that boy from Scotland Yard. Have you come across him? I can't believe he's old enough to be a detective. Anyway, it's difficult to work out where the boat went into the water because the Thames is tidal. You probably know this, but it's tidal all the way to Teddington Lock. That's a total of sixty-eight miles from the estuary out in the North Sea. The river can rise and fall by as much as twenty feet between tides. Sometimes more.

'On the night of the first of May, the low tide at London Bridge was at midnight. After that time, the tide came in and the river flowed upstream. High tide at London Bridge was around five o'clock the following morning. The second of May.'

'How fast does the river flow?'

'That varies. How long is a piece of string?'

'Can you give us a rough idea?'

'When the tide's coming in, the river can flow at seven knots, possibly as much as nine. Don't forget how much the Thames winds through London. There are some big bends on the river and it can flow faster on one side than on the other.'

'So, is it possible to know how far a boat like this would travel as the tide comes in?'

'No, not really. The boat could have been put into the water just about anywhere.'

'Deptford?'

'Yes, that's a possibility. It could even have gone in the water as far west as Richmond. But that's more unlikely, I'd say. When did I say it was high tide at London Bridge again?'

'Five o'clock on the morning of the second of May.'

'That's right. And after that, the river would have flowed downstream as the tide went out. I think low tide was just after midday on the second of May.'

'So when the boat was found at Chelsea at ten o'clock on the second of May, it had already travelled upstream for some time?' asked Augusta.

'Yes. And before that, it would have been carried downstream for some time.'

'So the boat was floating up and down the Thames,' said Philip. 'It could have ended up near where it started!'

'It could have done. And the reason it wasn't spotted sooner makes me wonder whether it spent some time stuck by one of the piers, jetties or bridge supports. It could have stayed somewhere like that for a while, hidden from view.'

'It's a shame we can't work out where this boat came from,' said Philip 'What's a boat like this used for?'

'What's it used for?' Inspector Tingle gave a bemused smile. 'It's a boat! It's used for travelling on water from A to B without you getting wet.'

'Very droll,' said Philip. 'I'm not really a boat person, so perhaps I didn't ask the question in the right way. What I mean is, who would have used this on the Thames? We're used to seeing big sailing ships, steamships, barges and that sort of thing. Would this little boat be used to take someone from the riverbank to a boat moored in the middle of the river perhaps? Or maybe a pleasure boat for someone to row at their own leisure? Not that I would like to take my chances rowing a little boat near all those big ones.'

'All of those things,' said the inspector.

'It looks just like the boats you can hire on the Serpentine in Hyde Park,' said Augusta.

'You're right, Mrs Peel. It's very similar. Just a plain old rowing boat. We don't know where it came from or who it belonged to. I wouldn't even waste time speculating, Mr Fisher.'

Augusta noticed Philip's jaw clench.

'But have you noticed something?' asked Inspector Tingle. 'There's no bullet damage in this boat. No holes or marks from any ricochets. We didn't find any shell casings either. I think the victim was shot before she was put into the boat.'

'On the riverside, you mean?'

'Yes. Or on a jetty or pier of some sort. Even in another boat. But I don't think she was shot while she was in this boat.' He gave it another kick. 'If only it could give up its secrets, eh?'

Chapter 40

'WELL, Inspector Tingle wasn't much help,' said Philip as he and Augusta travelled by taxi to Fleet Street. 'Let's hope the editor of the *London Weekly Chronicle* is more useful.'

'I DON'T UNDERSTAND why you're here,' said Mr Baker. He was a bald man with steel-rimmed spectacles. 'I've already spoken to Detective Sergeant Joyce from Scotland Yard.'

'I used to work at the Yard myself,' said Philip. 'But I work as a private detective now. I know Detective Sergeant Joyce well, and he's asked me to assist with the case.'

'Are you sure about that? I think I need to double-check this.' He glanced at Augusta. 'I'm rather confused by your presence as well, Mrs Peel.'

'Please feel free to telephone the Yard and check with them,' said Philip.

'I think I will. Do you mind?'

'Not at all.'

Augusta and Philip waited in the reception area of the

London Weekly Chronicle while Mr Baker went off for a few minutes. A sullen woman sat at the reception desk, her fingers dancing over the keys of a rapidly clacking type-writer. Framed front covers of the *Weekly Chronicle* hung on the walls. Augusta hoped Walter Ferguson wouldn't pass by and notice her here.

Eventually Mr Baker returned. 'I'm sorry for the inconvenience, but it appears you're both perfectly entitled to carry out this interview.'

They followed him to an office where papers were piled on every surface. A bookshelf behind the editor's desk bowed with the weight of heavy reference volumes on it.

'I'm afraid I don't have a lot of time,' said Mr Baker, settling behind his desk. 'Please tell me what you need.'

'First, I'd like to offer you my condolences on the loss of your staff member, Miss Ellen Foster,' said Philip.

'Thank you.' The editor blinked rapidly and his voice choked a little. 'We miss Ellen, I should say Miss Foster, very much indeed. It's a brutal and senseless act, and I can only hope the culprit is found and faces justice.'

'Do you have any idea who could have been behind it?'

Mr Baker gave a dry laugh. 'I had hoped the police would have found out by now, but it seems not. Obviously, I've given this question a lot of thought. We published a series of articles about the tin box factory in Deptford which is owned by the Stevenson family. We were concerned about the accidents being covered up there. It would be wrong of me to point the finger, because I have no evidence. But it would also be foolish if I didn't admit to you that the owner of the factory has a motive for silencing Ellen. I sincerely hope that's not what's happened, because that puts all of us here in fear of our lives. It would make every reporter on Fleet Street too frightened to carry out their work. That's an awful thought, isn't it?'

'Did Miss Foster leave many papers or notes?' asked Philip.

'She was very diligent with her record-keeping and her notebooks and files are all stored here in the office. If you're looking for clues, however, I think you'll be disappointed. Your colleagues have already looked through them and didn't find much.'

'How did Miss Foster get on with her colleagues?' asked Augusta.

'Extremely well. She was well-liked and very professional.'

'Did you favour her over other reporters here?' asked Philip.

Mr Baker spluttered at the directness of the question. Then pushed his glasses up his nose as he recovered himself.

'Favour her? No. I'll admit to you she was my best reporter, though.'

'Did that cause resentment?'

The editor shook his head and gave a laugh. 'No! I showed Ellen no favouritism whatsoever. I gave her some challenging stories to report on, and that's because I knew she was capable of doing a good job on them. All our reporters are good at what they do, but some couldn't quite match the standard of Ellen. If they were resentful or envious of her for that, then I'm afraid that's an immature way to behave. I expect better from my staff.'

'Perhaps Ellen Foster was attacked by one of her colleagues?'

Mr Baker slammed a hand on his desk. 'Absolutely impossible! I refuse to believe anyone who works for this newspaper would do such a thing! I can't deny there's natural rivalry between reporters, and that's the same with every newspaper. But a member of my staff would never murder a colleague out of sheer jealousy. That would be quite ridiculous!'

'Your reporter, Walter Ferguson, has displayed some intriguing behaviour,' said Philip.

'Walter? What's he done?'

'He's written an article about Mrs Peel.'

'Ah yes. I think he finds Mrs Peel a very interesting character indeed. And you are interesting, Mrs Peel. There aren't many ladies in London who are booksellers and also investigate crimes. In fact, you're probably the only one! It was an interesting article for our readers, I think.'

'I can't imagine they were that interested in it at all,' said Augusta. 'I think Walter Ferguson wrote that article because I asked him some questions about Miss Foster. He didn't like me asking questions, so he wrote the article out of revenge.'

The editor gave another dry laugh. 'Quite ridiculous. Walter's not like that at all. I'll admit he's eccentric in his ways, but he's an extremely good reporter. I'm very happy with his work.'

'He should have given Mrs Peel an opportunity to respond to the article he'd written about her before it was published,' said Philip. 'And the War Office is going to take a dim view of the mention of British Intelligence during the war.'

Mr Baker sat back in his chair. 'Is this an interview about my murdered reporter, Mr Fisher? Or a grievance about the article? I don't have a lot of time left to speak to you. If you have any further questions you'd like answered, then I advise you to ask them now.'

'Did Miss Foster tell you much at all about her personal life?'

'Absolutely not. She wasn't the sort of lady who would do such a thing. Our relationship was purely professional.'

'How much did you know about her life outside of her work?'

'I knew she rented rooms in Clerkenwell, and that was it. She was clearly an unmarried lady because she was devoted to her work.'

'We believe there was a gentleman friend who she may have been courting. Did you hear anything about that?'

'None whatsoever.' His lips thinned. 'That sort of thing is none of my business.'

'Of course,' said Philip. 'As investigators, we need to find everyone who knew Miss Foster. We've heard about a possible gentleman friend, but we don't know his identity. So we'd be grateful for any help you or your staff can offer.'

The editor gave a sniff. 'You could try some of the pubs and cafes on Fleet Street. They're well-frequented by reporters out of hours and you'll find gossip there, I'm sure. Whether it's reliable gossip or not, I couldn't tell you.'

'Did Miss Foster have any favourite places she liked to visit?'

'She liked the quieter ones. Some of the larger establishments can get very busy indeed. I believe she dined regularly at the Belmont Restaurant on Fetter Lane.'

'We'll ask in there,' said Philip. 'Thank you for your time, Mr Baker.'

'You're welcome.'

The editor's lips thinned again and Augusta felt sure his eyes were damp behind his steel-rimmed spectacles.

Chapter 41

'FERGUSON!'

Walter looked up from his desk to see Mr Baker summoning him. 'A word, please.'

Walter joined the editor in his office. He hoped this wasn't a conversation about some edits. He took great pride in his work and hated it when Mr Baker made changes.

'I've just had a strange conversation with a private detective and the lady you've been writing about. Mr Fisher and Mrs Peel. I don't like them.'

'Me neither, sir.'

'I don't understand why two people who call themselves private detectives are working on the case. I telephoned an acquaintance at Scotland Yard and he confirmed they're officially assisting with it. Mr Fisher has recently left the Yard and, from what my contact tells me, his nose was put out of joint there. He was replaced by the Commissioner's son on his final case.'

'Oh dear. So he sulked?'

'Must have done. I suppose he envisages a more lucrative profession working as a private detective.'

'With a curious sidekick.'

'Yes, very curious. They raised some curious points too. They suggested I showed some favouritism towards Miss Foster.'

Walter Ferguson frowned, keen to show this was a ridiculous idea.

'You don't agree with that suggestion?'

'No, I don't, sir. I don't think anybody thought you showed Miss Foster any favouritism.'

'Good. Well, that's a weight off my mind then. I don't like the way that pair invent things. Do you know they even suggested one of Miss Foster's colleagues could have attacked her?'

'Ridiculous!' spat Walter.

'Yes! That's what I said to them. I told them no one who works for me would ever have done such a thing.'

'Good.'

'I can't deny I was fond of Ellen,' said Mr Baker. 'I mean, Miss Foster. She was very good at what she did, wasn't she?'

Walter felt a bitter taste in his mouth. 'Yes.'

'I respected her enormously, and I thought she was a very capable reporter.' Mr Baker lifted his spectacles and wiped his eyes with his handkerchief. 'Oh I do apologise, Ferguson. I struggle to talk about her sometimes. It's no secret I was fond of Ellen. But I would be mortified if someone were to think I treated her more favourably than the rest of my reporters. You always worked well with her, didn't you, Ferguson?'

'I did, sir.' He gave a sincere nod to reassure the editor this had been the truth.

But it wasn't the truth. Baker had been infatuated with

Miss Foster, and everyone had known it. No one could do their job properly with that sort of thing going on. But how had Fisher and Peel worked it out? The last thing they needed was the police suspecting someone at the *Weekly Chronicle* could have been responsible for Miss Foster's death.

'It sounds as though Mr Fisher and Mrs Peel have been trying to put silly ideas into your head, sir,' he said. 'This is the trouble when private detectives are involved with the case. Scotland Yard has certain standards and would never stoop so low. I'm surprised that a former detective of the Yard would come out with such nonsense.'

'Yes, so am I. I suppose they have to consider all possibilities, don't they? Not just the obvious ones. And it's only natural that everyone should be suspected. But I was a little perturbed to hear it and I wanted to ensure there was no truth in it whatsoever. Out of all the reporters here, I consider you the most senior reporter now, Ferguson. You've been here the longest and you know everyone in this office better than anyone else. So I trust your opinion and if you say there was no animosity borne towards Miss Foster, then I believe you.'

'Very good, sir.'

Walter Ferguson couldn't resist a smile. The editor trusted him and believed his every word. He was in a powerful position.

Chapter 42

IT WAS LUNCHTIME, and the Belmont Restaurant on Fetter Lane was busy. Augusta and Philip found a small table by the door.

'The menu looks good,' said Philip. 'I might have to order the sausages.'

Augusta glanced at the surrounding tables. Most of their fellow diners were men in suits. The conversation was loud and lively.

'This looks like the sort of place where journalists like to gather,' she said.

'And didn't Mr Baker say Miss Foster preferred quieter places? If this is quiet, then the other places must be rather rowdy.'

'I can imagine they are.'

A red-haired waitress arrived at their table to take their order. Augusta asked for a pork chop with apple sauce.

'Sausages, please,' said Philip. 'With potatoes, carrots and an extra-large serving of gravy. And while you're here, can I ask if you recall Ellen Foster visiting this restaurant?'

The waitress gave a sad nod. 'She was a regular here.

We all miss her.'

'Can you recall when you last saw her?'

'She came in here a lot. It might have been on the day she died, or the day before. I can't exactly remember which it was. I didn't serve her that day, one of my colleagues did. But I served her many times, and she was a nice lady. Quiet, but always polite. And a nice change from some of the loud-mouthed reporters you get in here.'

'Did she come here alone or with friends and colleagues?'

'Both. Sometimes she came in here on her own and joined someone else at their table. Sometimes she came here with other people too.'

'I should explain that we're private detectives and we're working on the case.' Philip put a hand in his pocket. 'Here's my card.'

'Oh.' The waitress stared at it for a moment. 'I've never met a private detective before.'

'We've heard a rumour that Ellen Foster may have been courting someone. We can't be certain about it, but we need to do our best to investigate it. Were you aware of any gentlemen she enjoyed the company of?'

'Well…' The waitress looked out of the window as she thought. 'I suppose there's Simon Tennant.'

'Who's he?'

'A reporter at *The Daily Messenger*. I don't know if they were courting, but they came in here a lot together. He might know something.'

'Thank you very much. You've been far more helpful than anyone else we've spoken to today.'

'Really?' The waitress grinned. 'Well, I hope you catch the person who did it. And I'll ask the cook to make sure you get an extra-large serving of gravy.'

'You're very kind.'

Chapter 43

AUGUSTA AND PHILIP visited the offices of *The Daily Messenger* after lunch. The receptionist told them Simon Tennant was currently reporting on a case at the Old Bailey Central Criminal Court.

'It's probably the Huntingdon case,' said Philip.

'Dr Huntingdon who's suspected of poisoning his wife?'

'Yes. That's the case all the reporters will be interested in at the moment. It won't take us long to walk there. Shall we go?'

A SHORT WHILE LATER, Augusta and Philip squeezed themselves onto the packed benches of the public gallery in court number one.

'It's nice to be back here again,' whispered Philip. 'I always enjoyed attending the trials.'

The court room was a dull, high-ceilinged, wood-panelled room with the dock in the centre. Dr Huntingdon sat with his back to the public gallery, head held high. The judge, in gown and wig, sat at a raised desk opposite him. He was listening intently to a police constable answering questions from Dr Huntingdon's barrister.

The public gallery was situated up high at the back of the courtroom. From its commanding position, Augusta had a good view of the jury and the reporters on the press bench. She scanned the reporter's faces and spotted a dark-haired man of about thirty. He matched the description the landlady had given them.

They spent an interesting afternoon listening to Dr Huntingdon's barrister trip up just about everyone who stepped into the witness box.

'Dr Huntingdon's clearly hired the very best,' whispered Philip. 'He'd better not get off, that would be a travesty. There's no doubt the man's guilty.'

The court was adjourned shortly after four o'clock and it took a while for everyone to file slowly out. Augusta shuffled with the crowd and gritted her teeth with frustration. Hopefully they wouldn't miss their opportunity to speak to Simon Tennant.

They were able to apprehend him outside on the street. He had just skipped quickly across the road and been about to disappear down Fleet Place when Philip called out to him.

The reporter walked cautiously over to them. 'What is it?'

'Simon Tennant?'

'Yes. What do you want?'

'I'm a private detective, Mr Philip Fisher. And this is my colleague, Mrs Augusta Peel. We're assisting Scotland Yard with the investigation into the murder of Miss Ellen Foster. I believe you knew her, is that right?'

Mr Tennant scowled. 'I've got nothing to say.'

'That won't sound good when I report back to Scotland Yard. It's in your interests to be helpful.'

The reporter glanced around him. 'Not here,' he muttered. 'I'll see you in the King Lud pub in ten minutes.'

They watched him walk away.

'He's got something to hide,' said Augusta. 'Let's hope he turns up.'

Chapter 44

THE KING LUD public house occupied a prominent position at the crossroads of Ludgate Circus. The interior was furnished with elegant carved wood, gold-etched mirrors and ornate lamps.

Simon Tennant joined Augusta and Philip at a table. His hands trembled as he lit a cigarette.

'What's this about? Am I in trouble for something?'

'I don't know,' said Philip. 'We're here to find out. We've discovered Ellen Foster was courting with a gentleman shortly before her death. Was that gentleman you?'

'We were friends.'

'And have you spoken to the police about Miss Foster?'

'No, I haven't. Because our friendship wasn't common knowledge.'

'You call it a friendship. Was it a love affair?'

'I suppose so. But only for a short while.'

'Why the secrecy?'

He blew out a cloud of smoke. 'Perhaps you'd like to make an educated guess?'

'You're married?' said Augusta.

Mr Tennant sat back in his chair and said nothing.

'We'll take that as a yes.'

He leaned forward again. 'No one can find out about this.'

'Is that why you haven't come forward to the police?' asked Philip.

'Am I obliged to?'

'No, you're not obliged to. But you must have some information which can help them. And presumably, because you cared about her, you would want to do all you could to help the police find her murderer.'

'Yes, of course I do. But it's not that simple.'

'Because you were having an affair with her and you don't want anyone to find out. Least of all your wife. The police can be discreet, you know.'

He gave a laugh. 'I don't believe that for one minute.'

'You're a news reporter. You report on criminal cases such as the one you've attended in the Old Bailey today. Surely you know how crucial the smallest piece of information can be in an investigation. To remain silent suggests you're hiding something.'

'I'm merely hiding our relationship. Nothing more sinister than that.'

'When did you last see Miss Foster?'

'We met after work on the day she died.'

'And what time was that?'

'It was about a quarter past six. We went to the West End for a drink.'

Augusta was pleased to hear this. It was later than the last sighting they previously had.

'Where did you go for a drink?' asked Philip.

'The Dog and Duck in Soho.'

'And did you go anywhere else?'

'No. I had to leave at eight.'

'You had to go home to your wife?'

'Well, I think that's quite obvious.'

'So you last saw Miss Foster at eight o'clock in the Dog and Duck pub.'

'We said goodbye at the bus stop.' He bowed his head and rubbed at his brow as if hiding his emotion. Augusta tried to deduce whether the gesture was genuine or not.

'Where did she catch the bus from?'

'Shaftesbury Avenue.'

'And did you see her get on the bus?'

'No. I had to dash off.'

'So you don't know for certain that she got on the bus?'

'No. But I'm sure she would have done. She always did.'

'Your visit to the pub was a regular arrangement?'

'Yes, it was. We met there at least once a week. Then she got the bus back from Shaftesbury Avenue and I got the train home.'

'So on this occasion, did she mention she was planning to meet anyone else?'

'No. All I knew was that she intended to go home. So I don't know what happened. Perhaps someone abducted her? I don't know how, it's a busy street. You can't exactly pull up in a motor car and drag someone off the street in front of everyone else. But maybe that's what happened? I really don't know. I wish I did, but I don't.'

'What time did you get home that evening?'

'Half-past eight.'

'And your wife can vouch for that?'

'If you were to ask her, she would. But I urge you not to. If she's asked to provide an alibi for me, then she's going to find out about the affair. And she absolutely can't!

No one knew about it, and my marriage will be over if you tell her.'

He stubbed his cigarette out in the ashtray and lit another.

'How was Ellen when you saw her that evening?' asked Philip.

'She was her usual self. She was happy, and she enjoyed her work. She lived for her work and that's why our relationship suited her. She would have preferred me not to be married, but we couldn't help that.'

'Did she want you to leave your wife?'

'No. Well, I don't think so. Like I say, I don't think she liked the fact I was married.'

'Were you planning to leave your wife?'

'No.'

A pause followed.

'I know how it looks,' said Mr Tennant. 'I'm not claiming to be perfect.'

'Was Ellen concerned or worried about anything?' asked Augusta.

'If she was, she didn't mention it to me.'

'Had she received any threats?'

'Not that I know of.'

'Some people think she upset the owners of the factory she was reporting on.'

'It's an obvious one, I suppose. But a little too obvious, isn't it? I shouldn't think James Stevenson would risk that. And what has he got to lose? Nothing. Even if his factories are criticised in some newspaper reports, he's still inordinately rich, isn't he? He still lives the lifestyle he wants.'

'Have you ever met him?'

'Once. He's a typical spoiled young man.'

'So you don't think he could have been behind Miss Foster's murder?'

'I really don't know, Mrs Peel. Clearly Ellen had come across something she shouldn't have, and it angered someone. I really don't know what. She didn't tell me everything about her work. After all, we worked for rival newspapers. If she got a new story, she wouldn't always tell me immediately. She would wait until she'd done some work on it before she shared it with me. Then I'd have to play catch up!' He smiled. 'We had a friendly rivalry. And now she's gone, I have to pretend she meant nothing to me. I can't mourn or grieve. I can't attend the funeral. I have to suffer in silence.'

'You can help us find who did this,' said Augusta.

'I've told you all I know.' He got to his feet. 'Please don't come looking for me again.'

Chapter 45

'I THINK we need to speak to James Stevenson today,' Augusta said to Philip in her shop the following morning.

'Yes we do. I expect you're excited at the thought of seeing your friend again.' He smiled.

'Mr Toad of Toad Hall? Not likely.'

Philip laughed. 'I have to meet with Mr and Mrs Dashwood this morning. Mr Dashwood has left hospital and they've invited me to visit so they can say thank you. I don't know what they're thanking me for because I didn't really do anything.'

'You were extremely helpful and supportive during a difficult time. That's what she said, wasn't it?'

'It was something like that. I shall see you later, Augusta.'

AUGUSTA AND FRED spent part of the morning dusting and tidying the books.

'I forgot to tell you something, Augusta,' said Fred. 'Guess which book I sold yesterday.'

'Not *The Moonstone*?'

'Yes! For ten shillings.' He grinned. 'You could put more of the prices up, you know.'

'I'm pleased it sold for ten shillings. Thank you for persuading me, Fred. Perhaps I could put you in charge of pricing?'

'Yes, why not? I'd be happy to do that.'

The bell on the door rang as it opened. A customer stepped into the shop and Augusta's heart sank when she saw it was Walter Ferguson from the *London Weekly Chronicle*.

'I thought we agreed to stay out of each other's way?' she said. She held a feather duster in her hand which she felt tempted to hit him with.

'I thought that too,' he said. His red moustache gave a twitch. 'But then I heard you and Mr Fisher were in our offices yesterday speaking with my editor, Mr Baker.'

'That's right. Scotland Yard has asked us to assist with the investigation into Ellen Foster's death.'

'It's a shame you felt the need to tell him lies about the supposed rivalry between the reporters on the *Weekly Chronicle*.'

'Is there no rivalry at all between the reporters?'

'Absolutely not. You and Mr Fisher are stirring up trouble.'

'That's a rather dramatic way of describing it, Mr Ferguson. All we did was ask Mr Baker if there was any truth behind the rumours. He didn't think there was.'

'No. And he's absolutely right. And I don't see why that should be relevant when you're supposed to be investigating the murder of Miss Foster.'

'Because there's always the possibility that she was murdered by a colleague.'

'There's no possibility at all! If you and Mr Fisher are both investigators, you should be able to differentiate between facts and rumours. Repeating gossip to someone you're supposed to be interviewing isn't a professional way of going about things.'

'Is this the reason you're here, Mr Ferguson? To lecture me about how to conduct an investigation?'

'I'm here to speak on behalf of my editor who was most perturbed to hear reports of disharmony in our newsroom.'

'Is there anything else I can help you with, Mr Ferguson?'

'I wonder if you had a chance to read the article I wrote about you in the *Weekly Chronicle*, Mrs Peel.'

'The article in which you repeat rumours, Mr Ferguson?'

'Everything in that article was properly checked.'

'Well, I think it was a waste of ink. I shouldn't think any of your readers were the slightest bit interested in it.'

'On the contrary, I think you're exactly the sort of character our readers are interested in. I thought it would be courtesy to let you know that another article will be printed about you in the next edition.'

Augusta felt a ball of anger in her stomach. 'What a complete and utter waste of your time.'

'Not at all. This one is going to be rather more interesting. I've discovered more about your time in Belgium.'

'My work as a nanny there?'

He laughed. 'You and I both know that was your cover story. I've discovered what really happened.'

'Much of it is classified information. Your newspaper could find itself in trouble with the government.'

'I'm an experienced journalist. I know what's allowed. I think the public will be interested in reading all about Sarah.'

'Sarah?' Augusta felt the blood drain from her face.

'I thought that might shock you.' Ferguson's red moustache gave a satisfied twitch and he left.

Chapter 46

'THAT MAN IS INSUFFERABLE!' said Philip. They were travelling by taxi to James Stevenson's home in Mayfair and Augusta had just told him about Walter Ferguson's visit. 'How I would love to break his nose. I'm not a violent man, as you know, Augusta. But I swear he would drive me to it!'

'I wish I had never waited outside his office now. If only another colleague of Miss Foster's had stepped out instead. He seems determined to put me in my place.'

'Yes, he does. And why is he planning to publish a second article about you? I can't believe his editor Mr Baker allows him to do it.'

'He says the second article will mention Sarah.'

'What? He can't. Who's he talking to?'

'I don't know. I think he must know someone at the War Office who's giving him information.'

'He must do. I don't see how else he can find these things out. But writing about Sarah... that's all wrong.'

'Maybe he's just trying to worry me. Maybe he doesn't know much at all.'

'But he knows her name. He's got that from some-where. Do you know what I think, Augusta? He wants us to get worked up about it. That's why he's doing this. We shouldn't allow him to provoke us.'

'You're right.' Augusta took a breath to calm herself, but it didn't work. 'Ferguson has a vendetta against me. And I think he had a vendetta against Ellen Foster, too.'

'I agree. His behaviour is sinister and compulsive. Do you know what I'm going to do? Persuade a friend to speak to him.'

'Who?'

'A large, intimidating police constable who will give him an uncomfortable time.'

JAMES STEVENSON'S butler made them wait in the hallway of the grand Mayfair townhouse. The floor was tiled in a black and white chequered pattern. A chandelier hung above their heads and a grandfather clock ticked solemnly by the staircase.

'Mr Stevenson states he will only speak to you with Mr Grimston present.'

'Very well,' said Philip. 'How long will it take him to get here?'

'About ten minutes, sir. His office is a short distance away on Pall Mall.'

'Excellent, we're happy to wait.'

HALF AN HOUR LATER, they sat in Mr Stevenson's ostentatious drawing room on the first floor. The curtains and chairs and walls were covered in gold brocade. Street noise drifted in from a set of open double doors leading to a balcony.

Mr Grimston was a thin, pale-faced man with wispy grey hair. His cold eyes blinked slowly in a lizard-like manner. Augusta didn't like him one bit.

'You're lucky I'm agreeing to meet with you,' said James Stevenson. He smelled of too much cologne, and his face was puffy as if he had overindulged the previous evening.

'We're lucky?' said Philip.

'Yes. I have every right to refuse to meet with you after Mrs Peel accosted me in the club the other evening.'

'Accosted you? Do you know the meaning of the word? I believe she asked you a couple of questions in an exchange which lasted little longer than a minute.'

'Let's keep this conversation calm and civil,' said Mr Grimston. 'Now, what can we help you with, Mr Fisher?'

Philip explained they were assisting Scotland Yard with the investigation into Miss Foster's death.

'So, the Yard are struggling, are they?' James Stevenson grinned. 'They don't know who did it. And once again, everyone's hassling me about it. I've already told them what I know. I don't feel the need to repeat myself to you here today.' He turned to his companion. 'Grimston, you deal with them.'

Mr Grimston's lizard face remained impassive.

'Very well,' said Philip. 'Mr Grimston, did you ever meet Miss Ellen Foster, the news reporter for the *London Weekly Chronicle*?'

'No, I didn't,' he said. 'And neither did Mr Stevenson. Neither of us knew her.'

'And yet you must have been concerned about the articles she was writing about the factory?'

'Only mildly concerned. If there's one thing some of these local rags can't stomach, it's someone who's successful. Mr Stevenson comes from a distinguished family who are quite accustomed to this sort of criticism. I had a few words with the editor of the *Weekly Chronicle* and attempted to establish the motivation behind publishing the articles. I should add that the claims in them are completely unfounded. We had a polite conversation, but I regret he continued to allow one of his reporters to write inaccurate stories. It was unfortunate, but Mr Stevenson's business has many other priorities. It really didn't trouble us at all.'

'Which is why I don't understand why people think I had something to do with her death!' said Stevenson. 'As Grimston has just said, her stories didn't trouble us. It's annoying when lies are printed about my factories, but Grimston had a word with the editor and that was the end of it. Why would I risk everything by deciding to murder a news reporter? And how would I do it? I didn't even know what she looked like!'

'Mr Stevenson is quite right,' said Mr Grimston. 'And lies are often printed about successful people.'

'They certainly are,' said Philip. 'This is a complicated case, and I realise you don't like being accused of having been involved with the murder of Miss Foster, Mr Stevenson. The attack on the factory worker who spoke to Miss Foster is concerning, though. Surely this must have been something the factory management requested?'

'With regret, I believe it is,' said Mr Grimston. This admission surprised Augusta. 'It seems some ruffians at the factory took matters into their own hands. They have all been firmly spoken to, and I can assure you that something of this nature will never take place again. Mr Stevenson is going to visit the family and apologise to them.'

James Stevenson gave Grimston a sharp glance, as if this was the first he had heard about the plan.

'We take this sort of thing very seriously in our business,' continued Grimston. 'And there is absolutely no cause for anyone to take matters into his own hands.'

'Thank you for the admission,' said Philip. 'I trust you're going to give the police the names of the men you describe as ruffians.'

'Indeed we will.'

'Good. I'll inform Inspector Mansfield at Deptford police station he can expect to hear from you. You must have been annoyed yourself that Miss Beaumont spoke to the news reporter?'

'Not annoyed, no. The young woman was unduly concerned about safety standards at the factory. She spoke to her supervisor who rightly dismissed her claims as unfounded. It's extremely regrettable she felt the need to go to a newspaper about it.'

'Miss Beaumont told me she wrote a letter to Mr Stevenson expressing her concerns,' said Augusta. 'But she never received a reply.'

'I never saw her letter,' said James Stevenson. 'My correspondence is dealt with by my secretary.'

'I'm quite sure that if James Stevenson's secretary had received such a letter, then he would have brought it to my attention,' said Mr Grimston. 'There appears to have been a misunderstanding between Miss Beaumont and the management at the factory. It is something we'll look into.'

'So you admit you were responsible for the attack on Miss Beaumont? But you had nothing to do with Miss Foster's murder?'

'Not personally responsible for the attack on Miss Beaumont,' said Mr Grimston. 'I fear you are misinterpreting my words, Mr Fisher. I explained to you that a rough element at the factory meted out their own justice. They are very loyal to the factory and felt it was very damaging for Miss Beaumont to be speaking to the newspapers. Both Mr Stevenson and I do not endorse their actions, nor did we know what they had been planning to do. So, the men will be punished and we will apologise to the family. As for the attack on Miss Foster, we had nothing to do with it.'

'So the same ruffians who attacked Miss Beaumont didn't attack Miss Foster?'

'Absolutely not.'

'And how sure can you be of that?'

'The nature of the attacks was very different, Mr Fisher.'

'That's your evidence?'

Grimston gave an impatient sniff. 'Look, haul them in if you like and question them. But it will be a waste of your time. If you want to find out who murdered Miss Foster, you're looking in the wrong place.'

'Very well.' Philip turned to Stevenson. 'In the meantime, Mr Stevenson, I'd like to thank you for your cooperation so far. I have a request which I make of everyone we are speaking to, and that is to know your whereabouts on the night of the first of May.'

'How do I know what I was doing then?'

'It was the night when Miss Foster was murdered.'

'Here we go again. Despite everything Grimston has told you, you're still accusing me of murder?'

'No, I'm not. As I've already explained, it is a routine enquiry to establish the whereabouts of everyone on that evening.'

'Fine,' said Stevenson. 'Rita Crawford is your woman. I was with her. She'll tell you everything you need to know.'

Chapter 47

'EXCUSE THE MESS, I've just moved in,' said Rita Crawford as she showed Augusta and Philip into her top floor Mayfair apartment. The air was stale, and clothes were flung over the backs of chairs. Paintings were propped up against the walls, and books and newspapers sat in untidy heaps on the floor.

Miss Crawford looked like she had just got out of bed. She wore a violet silk robe over silk pyjamas and was barefoot. She smoothed her tousled bobbed hair with her hands and lit a cigarette. Despite her dishevelled appearance, Miss Crawford was still impressively beautiful. Her height and long limbs gave her a natural elegance.

'Goodness, this is unexpected!' She smiled and gestured for them to sit. Augusta perched next to a cat which was sleeping on a fur coat. It was difficult to see where the cat ended and the coat began.

Philip moved some books from an ornate chair and sat down.

'Have you got a bad leg?' Miss Crawford asked him.

'I wouldn't describe it as bad. I injured it during the

war, and it's taking some time to heal. In fact, I don't think it'll ever quite heal.'

'So you'll always need the walking stick?'

'Yes, I think so.'

'But that's so sad!' She flopped into an armchair and sat sideways with her long legs flung over the arm.

'You must excuse my appearance. I sleep so badly. I finally dozed off at ten o'clock this morning. What's the time now?'

'Two o'clock,' said Philip.

She sighed. 'What a dull middle-of-the-day time.'

'James Stevenson suggested we speak with you,' said Philip.

'Jimmy? How is he?'

'He seems well. As far as I can tell.'

'When did you see him?'

'We've just called on him.'

'I can't remember if he was there last night or not.' She pressed a palm into her eye. 'I get these awful blackouts. I suppose I should see a doctor about them.' She inhaled on her cigarette and angled her chin at the ceiling to puff out a cloud of smoke. 'Who are you again? Detectives, did you say?'

'That's right,' said Augusta. 'We're assisting Scotland Yard with the investigation into the murder of the news reporter Ellen Foster.'

'Oh, yes, I heard about that. Terrible.'

'We're trying to establish Mr Stevenson's whereabouts on the night of the murder.'

'You think he did it?'

'We're trying to find out the whereabouts of many people on that evening,' said Philip. 'Mr Stevenson is merely one of several people who had a connection to

Miss Foster. It's standard procedure to establish an alibi for everyone. He's not under suspicion at the moment.'

Augusta thought Philip's words were wise. She could imagine Rita Crawford being uncooperative if she thought they suspected James Stevenson of murder.

'Can I ask what you were doing on the night of the first of May?'

'What I was doing? Well, I was probably with friends. I see my friends every night.'

'Can you remember specifically what you did on that evening?'

'No, I don't think I can.' Miss Crawford puffed on her cigarette as she thought. 'I think we were probably at The 99 Club. And if I remember rightly, I think that was the evening we all got horribly bored, and we came back here.'

'When you say "we", who exactly do you mean?' asked Philip.

'Me and my friends. So there was, let me see...' She reeled off a list of names which Philip hurriedly tried to copy down into his notebook. 'And of course, there was Jimmy as well. I feel sure he was here that evening.'

'And what time did everyone come here?'

'I wouldn't know. We probably got to the club around half-past eleven. And then we decided it was boring, so we were probably only there for an hour. And then we all came here.'

'So at half-past twelve, perhaps? One o'clock?'

'Something like that.'

'And James Stevenson was in the club with you?'

'I think so.'

'You *think* so?'

'Yes. You know what it's like when you go to these places, Mr Fisher.' She paused and looked him up and down. 'Maybe you don't, actually.'

'Are you suggesting I don't know how to go out in the evening and have fun, Miss Crawford?' He gave a wry smile.

'Oh no. I hope you don't think I was suggesting that. I don't know, you see, whether you're the sort of person who likes to go to parties.'

'I love parties. I just don't get invited to them very often.'

'Well, then you must come to some of mine!' She giggled.

'So you think James Stevenson was with you throughout the evening of the first of May, but you can't be sure.'

'Yes. Because we had some drinks in a bar, and we went to the club, and there was a big group of us, so people were coming and going all the time. I think Jimmy was there for most of the time. In fact, I'm sure he was.'

'And he came back here to your apartment.'

'Yes. But I have to be honest with you, Mr Fisher, my memory is a bit hazy. It's the drink, you see. I don't drink very much. It only takes a few glasses for me to lose all sensibilities.'

'Did you ever meet Miss Ellen Foster?'

'The lady who died? No, I never met her at all. I don't have anything to do with news reporters.'

'Do you speak to them when they're writing for magazines like *Aristo*?' said Augusta.

'Oh yes, but that's different. I don't speak to actual news reporters, the ones who report on the news. I don't have any interest in news.'

'Did James Stevenson ever mention Miss Foster to you?'

'No, I don't think so. But sometimes he can be a bit of a bore, so I don't always listen to every word he says.'

'Perhaps he expressed concern that some critical articles were being written about one of his factories in the *London Weekly Chronicle*?' said Augusta.

'He might have done. I don't remember. Jimmy can be tremendous fun sometimes, but he can also be awfully tedious. I only tend to listen to him when I'm in the mood.'

'IT'S NOT EXACTLY a cast-iron alibi, is it?' said Philip once they had left Miss Crawford's apartment.

'Perhaps it's a ruse?' said Augusta. 'She's decided to cover for him but doesn't want to lie too much. So she says she thinks he was there, but she was too tipsy to remember for sure.'

'It's all a bit too convenient.'

Chapter 48

CONSTABLE BALLARD WAS the largest police officer Walter Ferguson had ever seen. He was over six feet tall, thick-shouldered, and had fists the size of hams. He stood in the centre of Walter's living room and refused to sit down.

'What do you mean by calling on me this early?' said Walter. He sat in his chair, gripping the arms. 'I haven't had my breakfast yet. I can't be late for work, you know.' His hip flask was in his pocket. He fought the urge to take it out and have a sip for courage. He had to show this man that he wasn't bothered by him at all.

The constable pulled out a notebook and pencil. They looked tiny in his enormous hands. 'What were you doing on the night of the first of May?' he asked.

'Why do you ask?'

Constable Ballard stared at him for a long time before answering. His jaw was the shape of an axe head. 'I'm the one asking the questions. Take my advice and answer them.'

'I was here. At home.'

'And who can vouch for that?'

'I would say my wife, but she was out at a committee meeting that evening.'

'So no one can provide you with an alibi?'

'My wife can provide an alibi.'

Constable Ballard scowled.

'Let me explain,' said Walter. 'I got home at about seven o'clock. My evening meal was being kept warm for me in the oven. I had my meal and then I sat down and did the crossword.'

'All very interesting, Mr Ferguson. But I want to know if there's someone who can vouch for the fact you were here that evening.'

'My wife returned at about ten o'clock.'

'She saw you here at ten o'clock?'

'Not quite.' A nervous laugh escaped from him. 'I wasn't here at ten o'clock. Sometimes I like to go to the pub on the corner for an hour.'

'So you went to the pub that evening?'

'Yes, I did. I completed the crossword and then, shortly before ten, I went to the pub.'

'Which one?'

'The Bull. It's the one on the corner.'

'So someone will be able to vouch for the fact you were in The Bull that evening?'

'Possibly. If they remember me. I didn't speak to anyone else in there, I just sat at a table in the corner. You could ask the landlord or one of the bartenders in there. They might remember me. Or might not. I'm not the sort of chap who stands out. It's possible no one made a note that I was there.'

Constable Ballard wrote in his notebook. 'I shall ask them all the same. Let's hope for your sake that someone does remember seeing you there. And what time did you leave The Bull?'

'Just after closing time. I got back here at half-past eleven.'

'And your wife will confirm that?'

'Yes… although she was already in bed by then.'

'Asleep?'

'Yes.'

'So you didn't see your wife at all that evening?'

'She was busy that evening, and when I returned, she was already asleep.'

'So she's not going to be much use as an alibi, is she?'

'She will tell you I ate the evening meal she left for me.'

'That's useful.'

'I should add my wife is away at her mother's at the moment, but she'll be back at the weekend so you can ask her then. If you think I had anything to do with Miss Foster's death, you're wrong.'

'You didn't like her very much, did you?'

'That's nonsense! I don't know where you've got that from.'

'It can't have been easy having a female colleague who was better at her job than you.'

'Now there's no need for that!' Anger made him spring to his feet. And he immediately regretted it because the constable towered over him. 'I won't have you standing in my house insulting me like that!'

'You've got a funny idea of what an insult is, Mr Ferguson. I was merely stating a fact.'

'Well, I don't know where you get your facts from, Constable, because that's complete and utter nonsense.'

'No doubt you were wondering where your future lay at the *London Weekly Chronicle*. The star reporter was better than you, and a lady too. You couldn't compete, could you?'

'I couldn't compete with the editor's affection, if that's what you mean. She wasn't as talented as everybody said she was. But Mr Baker was infatuated with her. This is the problem when women are allowed in the workplace.'

'You don't agree with it?'

'It causes problems. That's why women police officers don't do the same jobs that men do. You know all about that, of course. You and the women police officers do different things.'

'News reporters are not police officers, Mr Ferguson. And it seems you couldn't cope with a lady doing a better job than you.'

Walter clenched his fists. 'I find your manner impertinent! I shall report you to your superiors!'

'Very well.' The constable tucked his notebook and pencil away. 'I'm sure they'll be interested in hearing what you have to say for yourself. I've heard all I need to. I hope you enjoy your breakfast, Mr Ferguson. I'll show myself out.'

Walter's hand trembled as he took a large swig from his hip flask. He needed to provide an alibi for the first of May, otherwise he was in trouble. The only consolation today was that his second article on Augusta Peel was being published.

Chapter 49

AUGUSTA ARRIVED at the shop the following morning to find Philip and Fred leafing through a newspaper at the counter. As soon as she stepped through the door, Philip folded it up.

'What are you looking at?' she asked.

The two men exchanged a glance.

'One of you has to speak,' she said.

'Walter Ferguson's published his article,' said Philip.

She walked over to the counter and placed Sparky's cage on it. 'Does the article mention Sarah?'

Philip nodded and Augusta sighed. 'It shouldn't be reported in a newspaper,' she said. 'Let me read it.'

'Are you sure you want to?'

'Yes. I want to read something which has been written about me.'

'But it will make you angry.'

'And what's wrong with that?'

'Very well.' Philip opened the newspaper again. The headline read, "Secret Spy Story of Bloomsbury Bookseller." The article described how a woman named Sarah

Manford had vanished while working with Augusta and Philip in Belgium during the war.

'He's put Jacques's name in there, too,' said Augusta. 'How does he know about Jacques?'

Jacques Pero was a Frenchman who had worked with them in Belgium. He had visited Augusta recently to talk about Sarah's disappearance. He felt responsible for it, even though he wasn't.

'Ferguson is suggesting Sarah's disappearance was our fault!' said Augusta.

'Yes, he's implying we were careless in our jobs and that's why Sarah disappeared. To be honest with you, Augusta, he's not too far from the truth. But this information should not be public knowledge.'

'The only saving grace is that Sarah Manford wasn't her real name,' said Augusta. 'And I feel sure he's got no hope of finding out her true identity.'

Her heart felt heavy. Although they had known the risks when they had undertaken the mission in Belgium, Augusta still felt guilty about what had happened to Sarah. She had gone over the scenario many times in her mind, and she knew there was nothing more she could have done to prevent it. Their days in Belgium had been numbered once the German authorities grew suspicious of them.

Philip rested a hand on her shoulder. 'There was nothing more you could have done, Augusta. It was a dangerous time. We were in a dangerous situation. All four of us knew that. We knew the risks. Including Sarah.'

'I'm glad I wasn't there,' said Fred. 'I wouldn't have lasted longer than five minutes.'

'You're not giving yourself enough credit, Fred,' said Augusta. 'You would have lasted longer than that. But I can't deny they were tough times. I don't see why Ferguson feels the need to publish something like this.'

'Because he knows it upsets you,' said Philip. 'I'm going to speak to Mr Baker at the *Weekly Chronicle*. This can't continue.'

'Don't,' said Augusta. 'If you do, then Ferguson will know how much this bothers me. The best we can do is pretend we've not even read it. That will knock his inflated self-esteem. Do you know what will bother him the most? Being ignored.'

An enormous police constable filled the doorway.

'Who's this?' said Augusta, taken aback by the size of him.

'My good friend Constable Ballard!' said Philip. 'I think he's just paid Ferguson a visit.'

Augusta listened as the large constable told them about his conversation with Walter Ferguson.

'So he doesn't have a firm alibi for the night Ellen Foster was murdered?' she said once he had finished.

'No. I asked in the pub he said he'd been to. They know who he is there because he's a regular. But no one could confirm he had been in that pub between the hours of ten o'clock and half-past eleven that night.'

'So it's possible he was somewhere else,' said Philip.

'Meeting his colleague Ellen Foster in the West End, perhaps?' said Augusta.

'Possibly. The pair could have arranged to meet, or perhaps he followed her? Simon Tennant told us their meetings at the Soho pub were a regular arrangement. Maybe Ferguson knew that.'

'I don't think they arranged to meet because Mr Tennant told us he left her waiting at the bus stop. If she had been planning to meet with Ferguson, then presumably she would have mentioned it?'

'Good point,' said Philip. 'So perhaps Ferguson approached her at the bus stop.'

'And maybe he asked her if she wanted to have a discussion somewhere about a story one of them was working on.'

'Yes, he would have come with an excuse like that, wouldn't he? Then somehow found the opportunity to attack her. Simon Tennant says he left her at the bus stop at eight o'clock and we think she was murdered between ten o'clock and midnight. That gives us a gap of a couple of hours to fill.'

'He managed to keep her talking somewhere,' said Constable Ballard. 'The boat and gun were probably stored and ready somewhere on the riverside.'

'Yes!' said Philip. 'He could have found the boat somewhere and hidden the gun in it underneath the tarpaulin. If that's the case, then the boat must have gone into the water quite close to the West End. I think we could be looking at a stretch of the river between Westminster Bridge and Temple Pier.'

'Sounds sensible, sir,' said Constable Ballard.

'We should consider the south bank of the river,' said Augusta. 'It's easier to access the river from there. On the north side you have the wall of the Victoria Embankment and just a few access points.'

'I agree,' said Philip.

'And don't forget the river police station by Waterloo Bridge,' said the constable. 'He wouldn't have wanted to attack her under their noses.'

'And I agree with that too,' said Philip. 'We need a map which we can mark the most likely locations on. Can you suggest to Detective Sergeant Joyce that he puts some men on this, Ballard? They need to be knocking on doors in that area of the riverside. Perhaps Ferguson took Miss Foster to a pub or restaurant in that area. If we can find a witness who saw them together, then we could be onto something.'

The ring of the telephone interrupted them. Augusta answered and a voice at the other end introduced himself as Inspector Tingle from the river police. He asked to speak to Philip.

Augusta could tell something serious had happened as she listened to the conversation.

'Interesting,' said Philip once the telephone call had ended. He replaced the receiver and turned to Augusta. 'James Stevenson was attacked last night.'

Chapter 50

'ATTACKED?' said Augusta. 'Is he dead?'

'No. Stevenson survived and is being treated in St Thomas's Hospital.'

'So what happened?'

'He was attacked on Waterloo Bridge and thrown into the river.'

'By who?'

'They don't know. Witnesses are being sought, and hopefully we'll know some more soon. The attack happened in the early hours of this morning. Apparently, he was taking a night-time stroll when he was set upon. The motive doesn't appear to have been robbery. His watch and wallet weren't taken or even asked for. Apparently, the man told him he was for it.'

'Revenge for something?' said Augusta.

'It could be. Perhaps someone who was injured in an accident at his factory? Or perhaps it has something to do with Ellen Foster's murder. Apparently, the man approached him from behind, taking him by surprise. He was knocked to the ground, then kicked and punched and thrown over the wall of the bridge into the river.'

'He could have drowned!'

'He could have done. Fortunately for him, he was saved by a river police patrol boat. This seems like an attempt to murder him.'

'It has to be something to do with Ellen Foster's murder, don't you think?' said Augusta.

'I think it must be. There's been so much talk about James Stevenson being the murderer that perhaps someone has taken matters into their own hands and exacted revenge.'

'Or it was someone who wanted to silence Ellen Foster, then they wanted to silence him, too.'

'But they haven't quite succeeded, have they?'

Chapter 51

ANTHONY GRIMSTON APPROACHED the bench where Robert Stevenson sat waiting for him. Their meeting had been hastily arranged over the telephone only an hour earlier. Anthony took his place on the bench and admired the mature trees which lined the paths of Green Park.

'You've gone too far, Anthony,' said Robert. 'James could have died.'

'I had nothing to do with it.'

'Then who attacked him?'

'I don't know. But it wasn't me.'

Robert resembled his older brother, but he was a little leaner in the face. He pushed his hands into the pockets of his overcoat and sighed. 'I don't believe you.'

'You don't believe me? But I've never lied to you, Robert. Why would I lie about this?'

'Because you've gone too far this time. I thought you went too far attacking the young woman. But to actually have James attacked? I didn't think you'd sink to that.'

'And presumably nothing I can say will convince you I'm completely innocent?'

'This wasn't how the plan was supposed to work.'

Anthony felt frustrated. He needed Robert's trust. 'I know that. This entire business was going to be carefully orchestrated. Slow and gradual, that's what we agreed.'

'But you got impatient and hurried things along by hiring someone to finish him off.'

'I didn't!'

'So who did?'

'I don't know. It's a mystery.'

'It can't just be a mystery. You must know something. Perhaps I should have known better than to trust you. You've double-crossed James, so you could just as easily double-cross me, too.'

'Where do you get that idea from?'

'Because it wasn't too difficult to persuade you to be disloyal to him. When I suggested we remove him as owner of the family business, you agreed.'

'Because he's incompetent!'

'You've proven to me you're not loyal.'

'My loyalty lies with the business. I can't bear to see everything so badly managed. Your father would have been horrified.'

'Yes, he would.'

'So I have never seen this as a betrayal of James. It's about having the best interests of the business at heart. Your father had four sons, but only three of them are capable of managing the business effectively. James has proven himself unworthy on that front, and that's why I agreed to support you. But it would be foolhardy of me to arrange an attack on James. We've known all along that his own actions will end him. Some shame committed while inebriated or a foolhardy public mistake such as an affair. But I can assure you I have never considered arranging for someone to attack him.'

'Maybe you attacked him yourself?'

'Me?' Anthony felt a snap of anger. 'I could just as easily accuse you, Robert! You've been waiting in the wings all this time. Perhaps it was you who attacked the reporter? After all, hoping to inherit the business, you would not want her writing the things she did about your family's company. And perhaps you got impatient with our plan? Perhaps it was you who attacked your own brother.'

Robert got to his feet. 'Well, it's clear we need answers,' he said. 'And fast. Otherwise, all trust is gone.'

Anthony Grimston watched him walk away.

Chapter 52

'MR STEVENSON HAS BEEN THROUGH AN ORDEAL,' said the nurse at St Thomas's Hospital. 'You can only spend a few minutes with him. He needs to rest.'

'Yes, I understand,' said Philip. 'We'll make this as quick as possible.'

Augusta and Philip walked through the ward to the bed where James Stevenson was propped up on thick, white pillows. His face was pale and bruised, and his body looked limp.

He sighed when he saw them. 'Not you again. I've already spoken to the police. I don't need you here as well.'

'Well, you know why we're here, Mr Stevenson,' said Philip. 'We need to find the man who did this to you.'

'I've told the police everything. I hardly saw him. He approached me from behind and I had no time to react. I wish I'd heard him sooner and turned around. I wish I could have fought back. I'd had a few drinks, so my reactions were slow. I just wasn't expecting it at all.'

'It sounds like there was nothing more you could have done.'

'No, I couldn't have done anything else. I'm just lucky the river police were close by so they could rescue me from the water.'

'Did your attacker speak to you?' Philip asked.

'Yes. He told me I was for it.'

'Can you describe his voice? Was he well-spoken? Roughly spoken? Any idea of an accent or his background?'

'Fairly well-spoken, I suppose. And he knew who I was. He must have been following me. I'd had some drinks, and I was taking a night-time stroll, I wasn't really paying attention to who was around me. Perhaps he followed me from the club, I don't know.'

'Would you recognise the voice if you heard it again?'

'I think so. And there was something about his voice which was familiar.'

'You'd heard his voice before?' asked Augusta.

'Yes... but maybe I'm just imagining it. He clearly knew me, though, so perhaps I have met him before and I just don't remember him very well.' He clasped his hand to his forehead. 'I keep getting these dreadful headaches.'

Augusta glanced along the ward to where the nurse was already approaching them. 'We should leave you to it, Mr Stevenson. It looks like the nurse is going to come to your assistance. Thank you for telling us all you can. You're lucky to be alive.'

'I am.'

'SO WHO COULD THE ATTACKER BE?' asked Augusta as they left the hospital.

'Well, let's consider the other suspects. Martha Beaumont. It can't have been her because Mr Stevenson says a man attacked him. That leaves us with Walter Ferguson.'

'Or Anthony Grimston.'

'Mr Grimston... now that's a thought, isn't it? It's possible he was behind Ellen Foster's murder. Perhaps he's behind this attack too?'

'But why?'

'Perhaps James Stevenson found something out. He was already upset to discover a factory worker had been attacked, and I think it's likely Mr Grimston asked those men at the factory to attack her. And if Mr Grimston was behind Ellen Foster's murder, perhaps he accidentally let something slip? Perhaps James Stevenson knows more than he should?'

'In which case, we're lucky he survived. Because he can now tell everything to the police, can't he?'

'Indeed, he can. I'll suggest to Joyce that he arrests Grimston. And if Stevenson learns Grimston is in custody, then he may be more willing to talk.'

Chapter 53

'I HAVE DUTIFULLY SERVED the Stevenson family for over thirty years,' said Anthony Grimston. 'Do you honestly think I would try to murder the heir and owner of the family business?'

He sat in a sombre interview room in Scotland Yard facing Detective Sergeant Joyce. Today was turning out to be the worst day of his career. Robert Stevenson had accused him of the attack and now the police were doing the same. Why did everyone think he was behind it?

'Mr Stevenson says he was attacked by a well-spoken man,' said Detective Sergeant Joyce. 'He says he thinks he recognises the man's voice.'

'And so that means it must be me? Has it not occurred to you that Mr Stevenson has many friends and acquaintances whose voices he would also recognise? Has he told you that the voice of the man who attacked him was me?'

'No.'

'Well, there's no reason for you to arrest me then, is there?'

'Maybe he doesn't want to admit it was you. Maybe he

doesn't like to think that a man he trusts would betray him in such a manner.'

'No, that's nonsense.'

'We suspect Ellen Foster's murderer could be the man who attacked James Stevenson.'

'Why?'

'Both attacks happened by the river at night.'

'That's your reason?'

'At the moment. We're still working on it, though.'

'And you think I'm capable of attacking both of them?'

'You had a strong motive for attacking Ellen Foster.'

'As did Mr Stevenson! And yet you don't suspect him?'

'You wanted to protect the business. You didn't like what Miss Foster was writing about the Deptford factory.'

'But I didn't murder her.'

'Perhaps Mr Stevenson discovered you murdered Ellen Foster?'

'No! Ridiculous.'

'Perhaps he accused you?'

Anthony responded with laughter. 'Have you thought about a career in writing fiction, Detective? I've never heard so much twaddle in all my life. And besides, I'm not the sort of man who hangs about on Waterloo Bridge in the early hours of the morning. It's no secret that Mr Stevenson is a night owl. He put himself at risk by wandering about late at night drunk.'

'Which made it all the easier for you to push him into the river, wouldn't you say?'

Chapter 54

'WHAT A DRAMATIC DAY,' Augusta said to Fred as they prepared to close the shop. 'Sometimes it feels over-whelming trying to keep up with it all. And I'm so behind on repairing books. Have you seen how big the pile is in the workshop now?'

'I have. But there's no hurry, Augusta. We still have lots of stock. By the way, I found some more photographs of James Stevenson and the Crawford sisters in *Aristo*. I don't know if you're still interested in searching for them but I wanted to complete the task.'

'Thank you, Fred. That's very thoughtful of you.' She hadn't the heart to tell him they had already found out what they needed to from *Aristo*.

'I've added the copies to the pile on the shelf under the counter.'

'I shall have a look at them. Oh no...' Someone stepped into the shop. 'Not Walter Ferguson again. I can't cope with the man. Would you mind going upstairs and asking Philip to join us? I'm not sure I can handle Ferguson by myself this evening.'

Fred went up the stairs and Ferguson stood in the centre of the shop with a smug expression.

'It seems you can't stay away,' said Augusta.

'Absolutely, Mrs Peel. I wonder if you have read this week's edition of the *Weekly Chronicle*?'

'No, I haven't.'

'You haven't?'

'No, I don't usually read the *Weekly Chronicle*. Is there anything interesting in it?'

'The second article has been published, Mrs Peel.'

'Why?'

'Because I thought our readers would find it extremely interesting. The story of Sarah Manford fascinated me.' Augusta's stomach flipped with anger. She nonchalantly picked up the bag of birdseed and began feeding Sparky. 'Well, I'm pleased it entertained you. It's a sad story, so I can't imagine it entertained your readers at all. Is there anything else I can help you with?'

To Augusta's satisfaction, Walter Ferguson seemed deflated. He had presumably hoped she would be angry with him.

'That was all. I thought I'd draw your attention to the article.'

'There were many good reasons why our work during the war remained top secret, Mr Ferguson. I just hope you haven't upset any of the other people mentioned in the article. Sarah's family, for example.'

'Do you know them?'

'No, I don't. But maybe they'll contact your editor about it.'

Augusta heard footsteps on the stairs.

'What are you doing here?' came Philip's voice from the stairs. 'Get out!'

'I beg your pardon?' said Walter Ferguson.

Philip reached the foot of the stairs, then headed straight for Ferguson. 'Get out of this shop at once! And don't return.'

'May I ask why you're so riled, Mr Fisher?'

'I don't have to explain myself to you. Just leave. If you're not careful, Constable Ballard will pay you another visit. I'm sure you don't want that, do you?'

'I might have thought you would ask your friends at the police to bully me, Mr Fisher. How cowardly.'

'Not half as cowardly as writing inaccurate articles about a good friend of mine. You've got five seconds to leave this shop, you nasty little worm.'

Ferguson backed away. 'Alright, I get your point, Fisher.'

'Out! Now!' Philip raised his stick and pointed it at the door.

'I'm leaving.'

'Good! And if you set foot in here again, I shan't be responsible for what happens to you!'

Chapter 55

AUGUSTA AND PHILIP visited Detective Sergeant Joyce at Scotland Yard the following morning.

'Within the hallowed walls again,' said Philip as they walked along a dingy, wood-panelled corridor. 'And back here much sooner than I thought!'

Joyce looked tired. The fairness of his skin accentuated the dark circles beneath his eyes. Augusta wondered if he was regretting becoming a Scotland Yard detective.

'I interviewed Anthony Grimston yesterday,' he said as they sipped tea at his desk. 'But I think I'm going to have to release him.'

'Why?' said Augusta. 'Surely he's the most likely person to have attacked James Stevenson?'

'He's adamant that he didn't.'

'Well, he would be,' said Philip.

'I'm struggling to find his motive. Why would he attack the man who employs him? As he explained, he's been loyal to the Stevenson family for over thirty years.'

'It seems he did a good job of convincing you.'

'He did. I realise he's the sort of man who can be quite persuasive, but I believe him.'

'I think the motive is that James Stevenson found out Anthony Grimston murdered Ellen Foster,' said Philip. 'So Grimston had to silence him. He probably ordered one of his ruffians to attack him, just as he did for the attack on Miss Beaumont.'

'The attacks seem similar,' said Joyce. 'But they're not completely the same. Two men attacked Miss Beaumont, but only one attacked Mr Stevenson. And besides, Inspector Mansfield in Deptford has arrested the two men who attacked Miss Beaumont. Mr Grimston gave him their names.'

'They were in custody at the time of the attack on Stevenson?'

'No, they were arrested yesterday.'

'So it's possible one of them attacked Stevenson.'

'I suppose so. But they've admitted to the attack on Miss Beaumont. If they were behind the attacks on Miss Foster and Mr Stevenson, then why not admit to those, too?'

'It's a tactic,' said Philip. 'You confess to the lesser crime, and then you seem like an honest chap who genuinely had nothing to do with a more serious crime. It seems to me though, Joyce, you're convinced Grimston is not our man.'

'No, I don't think he is. I realise I'm not as experienced as you, Mr Fisher. And I know people are questioning my ability to investigate this case. However, I believe I have some decent investigative skills, and I'm learning an awful lot as each day passes. My instincts tell me that Grimston is not the right man.'

'But James Stevenson said the voice of the man who attacked him sounded familiar,' said Augusta.

'Yes, but that doesn't mean it was Grimston,' said Joyce. 'And besides, isn't there a possibility that Mr Stevenson was mistaken about the man's voice? By his own admission, he was in a state of inebriation at the time.'

'That's a good point,' said Philip.

'If it's not Anthony Grimston, then what about Walter Ferguson?' said Augusta.

'Ferguson's motive for murdering Miss Foster was rivalry or jealousy of some sort,' said Philip. 'What could his motive for murdering James Stevenson be?'

'I don't know.' Augusta sighed. 'Perhaps there's a connection between the two men which we haven't uncovered yet.'

'It's worth looking into,' said Joyce, making a note.

'The only other person I can think of is Martha Beaumont,' said Philip. 'She has the perfect motive. Stevenson was behind the attack on her sister.'

'Stevenson claims he knew nothing about it,' said Joyce.

'I know, but he must have done,' said Philip. 'And I'm sure Miss Beaumont sees it that way. The only trouble is Stevenson maintains he was attacked by a man.'

'But he was drunk at the time,' said Augusta. 'And his assailant surprised him from behind. So perhaps he doesn't recall the attack correctly. Or maybe he knows it wasn't a man, and he's too ashamed to admit a woman attacked him and threw him into the river?'

'An ingenious suggestion, Augusta!' said Philip. 'I can imagine that being a possibility.'

'I'll interview Martha Beaumont again,' said Joyce. 'Let's see what she has to say for herself.'

Chapter 56

'YOU CAN'T LEAVE me alone, can you?' Martha folded her arms and glared at the young Scotland Yard detective and Inspector Mansfield. She was back in the spartan interview room at Deptford police station. 'You should have caught the murderer by now. Why do you keep harassing me?'

'James Stevenson was attacked on Waterloo Bridge,' said Detective Sergeant Joyce.

'Good.' She smiled. 'Is he dead?'

'No.'

'Shame.'

'Can you tell me anything about it?'

'No, I can't. The first I knew of it was when you told me about it just now. How can you expect me to help you?'

'I can understand why you might want to attack James Stevenson.'

'Yes, I would like to attack him. But it sounds like someone else got there before me.'

'So, you were planning to attack him?'

'Of course not. Where would it get me? I would only be arrested again.'

'Perhaps you asked someone to attack James Stevenson for you?'

'I don't think anybody in their right mind would attack a man just because I told them to. And I'd need money to pay them. I don't have any money.'

'Perhaps you persuaded a good friend?'

'I like to settle my own battles. That's how I do things. But I wouldn't waste my time with James Stevenson. Where would it get me?'

'Men from his factory attacked your sister,' said Inspector Mansfield. 'They've admitted it.'

'Good. You finally got them.'

'James Stevenson could have been the one who asked them to attack your sister.'

'Yes, he could have and that's why I don't like him. But I didn't try to murder him.'

'You were upset about what happened to your sister,' said Detective Sergeant Joyce. 'She was attacked because she spoke to a news reporter. It's not surprising you would want revenge for the people who harmed her.'

'I've already told you, I didn't do it!' Martha felt tired of being accused. Was it because it was easy for them to do it? She was a young woman with no money and a history of trouble. She had no power. All she could do was try to talk her way out of this. 'Revenge gets you nowhere,' she said. 'That's why I didn't attack him. I'm happy someone did, though.'

'I've been making some enquiries about you at the Mason's Arms,' said Inspector Mansfield.

Martha felt a cold lurch in her stomach. 'Why?'

'You've been working for the Armada Street Gang, haven't you?'

'Who are they?'

'Oh, come on, Miss Beaumont. Everyone in your part of Deptford knows who they are.'

She folded her arms even tighter. 'I don't know what you're talking about.'

He leant on the table and glared at her. 'There's no use in pretending. We know everything.'

A sense of panic rose in her chest. She had to remain calm. 'Like what?'

'I'm not going to disclose it all because our investigation is still ongoing. But I know you've been disposing of evidence for them.'

She scowled, keen to show this was nonsense. 'Like what?'

'Stolen items which became too hot to handle. Weapons which they don't want the police to find. That sort of thing.'

'Someone's been telling you a load of rubbish!'

'You like to throw it all in the river, don't you? You don't think anyone's going to find it again.'

'This is lies. You've got nothing on me.'

Inspector Mansfield examined some papers in front of him. 'We have reason to believe you recently disposed of a revolver. Perhaps you might like to explain why?'

'I've got nothing to say to you! Someone's trying to frame me. You can't keep me here any longer.'

She got to her feet and walked over to the door. She tried the handle, but it was locked.

In an explosion of rage, she punched the door. It was solid wood and painted with thick lacquer. Pain shot through her knuckles.

'Come and take a seat again please, Miss Beaumont,' said the inspector. 'You've got a lot of explaining to do.'

As Martha returned to her seat, there was a knock at

the door. Inspector Mansfield got up to answer it. Before he unlocked it, he pointed at Martha. 'Don't even think about trying to escape!'

Martha sneered at him. She would try again when they were least expecting it.

The caller at the door was a constable. 'Detective Sergeant Joyce,' he said. 'Your assistance has been requested. Shots have been fired at an address in Clapham.'

Chapter 57

AUGUSTA HAD JUST PUT Sparky to bed in his cage that evening when the telephone rang.

'Augusta, it's Philip. Fancy a trip to Clapham?'

'Now?'

'Yes.'

'Why?'

'Joyce has telephoned me. He investigated a shooting incident at a house in Clapham this afternoon. You'll never guess who lives there.'

'You'd better tell me then.'

'Our old friend Simon Tennant.'

Augusta gasped. 'The man who Ellen Foster was having an affair with?'

'Yes. His wife has been arrested for threatening him with a gun. No one has been hurt. Joyce isn't sure yet if the altercation has anything to do with Miss Foster, but he's asked if we can have a chat with Mr Tennant because we've spoken with him before.'

'Very well. Where shall I see you?'

'I'll get a taxi to yours now.'

. . .

SIMON TENNANT LOOKED a little more dishevelled than when they had last seen him. His collar had come loose and his hair was untidy. His eyes had a wide, haunted look about them. By contrast, the living room was neat and comfortably furnished. It was difficult to imagine it had been the scene of an unpleasant incident hours earlier.

'We're assisting Detective Sergeant Joyce of Scotland Yard,' said Philip. 'We understand your wife has been arrested after threatening you with a revolver and shots were fired.'

Mr Tennant nodded. 'Two shots.' He pointed to the hearthrug which had two holes in it.

'The gun was fired into the floor?'

He nodded again.

'Warning shots?'

'Something like that. She was very angry.'

'About what?'

'What do you think?'

'Your affair with Ellen Foster.'

'Yes.' He lit a cigarette.

'I've been told the gun is a Webley revolver,' said Philip. 'Was the gun kept in this house?'

'Yes. I didn't think we had any ammunition for it, but it turns out we did.'

'Did your wife find the ammunition and know how to load it into the gun?'

Simon Tennant shrugged. 'Apparently so.'

'How did she find out about the affair?'

'Apparently she'd been suspecting it for some time. I didn't realise that when I last spoke to you. I just assumed she knew nothing about it. But ever since Ellen's murder, I suppose my mood has changed a little. My wife must have noticed. Women can be quite observant of these things.'

'So she suspected it, but how did she actually find out?'

'She discussed it with friends. Quite astonishing really, I didn't think she'd want to tell anyone our business.'

'Presumably she was worried and needed to talk to someone about it,' said Augusta.

'I suppose so. The wife of a friend told her. I realise now my friendship with Ellen was fairly common knowledge on Fleet Street. People saw us together. And although we tried to create the impression we were merely colleagues, I suppose people suspected we were more than that. I have several personal friends who are news reporters, and my wife and I have socialised with them and their wives a lot in the past. That's how word got back to her.' He shook his head. 'It was foolish of me to think I could keep it a secret.'

'But why did she decide to confront you today?'

'Because she only found out about it this morning. She went shopping with the friend who told her. Then she telephoned me at work in a state of utter distress. I rushed back home and that's when she confronted me. I denied it initially and that seemed to make matters worse.'

'Having confronted you, your wife presumably expected you to have the decency to tell her the truth,' said Augusta.

'Yes, it wasn't very decent of me, was it? Anyway, she went upstairs to where the gun was kept in a box in the wardrobe. I don't know why I kept it in the house. I couldn't quite bring myself to get rid of it, I suppose. Maybe I kept it for self-defence purposes. Anyway, she came downstairs, and then she was pointing the thing at me.'

'Do you think she intended to kill you?'

'No. I think she just wanted to scare me. And it worked, of course. She fired the thing into the floor. Such a deafening noise!'

'How did the police become involved?'

'The neighbour called them when she heard the shots. Quite embarrassing, really. Now the entire street knows what has happened between us.'

'The revolver which your wife threatened you with is the same type of gun which was used in the murder of Ellen Foster.'

'Well that's not surprising.' Augusta was surprised by his calm response. 'They were standard issue during the war.'

'The same type of weapon was used, and yet you still deny having anything to do with Ellen Foster's death?'

'Absolutely.'

Augusta had a thought. 'Are you quite sure your wife only discovered Ellen Foster's identity this morning?'

'Yes, quite sure.'

'Can you remember what your wife was doing on the evening of the first of May?'

'Of course not. You'd have to ask her. Just a moment... Are you suggesting my wife shot Ellen Foster?'

Chapter 58

AUGUSTA AND PHILIP walked the short distance from the Tennant's house to the police station on a quiet residential street called Cavendish Road. It was a cool, clear evening and a late-night blackbird sang from a nearby tree.

'You think Mrs Tennant could have murdered Ellen Foster?' Philip asked as they walked.

'It's a possibility, don't you think? But only if she had somehow discovered Ellen's identity. And I'm not sure if I believe everything Simon Tennant told us.'

'What do you mean?'

'He says his wife threatened him with the gun after finding out about the affair. He says she did it to frighten him. But if she didn't intend to kill him, then why threaten him with a gun at all? Surely it would have been enough to confront him?'

'Maybe she wanted him to think she was going to kill him, and that's why she fired two shots into the floor.'

'Possibly, but it strikes me as an odd thing to do. Perhaps Mr Tennant is lying to us and it was he who threatened his wife with the gun. Perhaps that's how he likes to win his arguments. Maybe he shot Ellen Foster, and he intended to do the same to his wife. But fortunately, she was saved by the actions of the neighbour calling the police.'

'It's a possibility, Augusta. We've only heard one side of the story and it may not be reliable. Let's speak to Mrs Tennant and see what she has to say.'

THEY MET Detective Sergeant Joyce at the police station.

'How did you get on with Mr Tennant?' he asked.

'He described to us what happened,' said Philip. 'But we don't know whether to believe him or not. We'd like to speak to Mrs Tennant and find out if their stories match up.'

'Very well. I spent some time with her this afternoon and she was extremely distressed. Hopefully she's calmed down a little now, although I don't know what you'll get from her at this late hour.'

MRS TENNANT WAS a meek figure with slumped shoulders and mousy brown hair. She pulled her cardigan tightly around her and sat with her arms folded. There was something pitiful about her.

'Can you tell us how the argument with your husband began, Mrs Tennant?' asked Augusta.

'A friend told me about his affair with Ellen Foster. I was very upset.' She was well-spoken but quiet.

'So you confronted him.'

'Yes. I telephoned him at his office and asked him to come home. When he got home, I told him what I'd heard and asked if it was true.'

'And what was his reaction?'

'He denied it! He couldn't bring himself to tell me the truth. We've been married for fifteen years! And he couldn't be honest with me.'

'And that angered you?'

'I was more upset than angry.'

'At what point did you fetch the gun?'

'When I was very upset. I wasn't thinking straight. I just went upstairs, went to the wardrobe, took the gun out of its box and went back downstairs. Then I pointed it at him.'

'Did you know the gun was loaded?'

'I just assumed it was.'

'Why was it loaded?'

She shrugged. 'I don't know. I don't know much about guns. I just knew where it was kept. I didn't give much thought whether there were bullets in it or not.'

'You didn't give it any thought?' said Philip. 'But surely threatening someone with a loaded gun is much more effective than threatening someone with one which is unloaded?'

'All I know is that I was upset, and I pointed it at him. I wanted him to understand how upset I was.'

'Usually when a gun is stored, it's stored with no ammunition in it,' said Philip. 'It's much safer that way. Your husband says he didn't realise there was any ammunition in the house. He thinks you put the ammunition in the gun.'

'No, I didn't. It was already in there. I wouldn't know how to load a gun with bullets.'

'When did you fire the shots?'

'When I was upset.'

'And you fired them into the floor?'

'Yes.'

'Why?'

'To frighten him, like I said.'

'And did it work?'

'Yes, he sat down and was quiet.'

'Quiet?' said Augusta. 'So he had been noisy until that point?'

'Yes, he was shouting at me.'

'Shouting at you? Even though you were the one who was upset?'

'Yes. I suppose it got him upset too.'

'Do you and your husband argue often?' asked Philip.

'Occasionally.'

Something didn't feel right. Augusta spoke in her calmest, most sympathetic tone. 'Mrs Tennant, are you telling us the truth?'

She nodded.

'We need to know exactly what happened today. Are you sure you're not telling us a story designed to protect someone?'

She shook her head.

'If what you've told us isn't completely true, you can tell us, you know,' said Augusta. 'We can make sure you're safe.'

Mrs Tennant bowed her head and began to cry.

Philip went out of the room to fetch a police woman to look after Mrs Tennant. He and Augusta then spoke again with Detective Sergeant Joyce.

'There's something very odd going on here,' Philip said to him. 'I was surprised when Mr Tennant said his wife loaded the gun with ammunition. She's just told us she doesn't know much about guns!'

'And it's strange that she said she gave little thought to whether or not there were bullets in the gun,' said Augusta. 'Presumably, she believed there were, and that's why she threatened him with it.'

'So he maintains the gun was unloaded and she says it was loaded,' said Joyce.

'Exactly,' said Augusta. 'I suspect she's telling us a story that he has asked her to tell us. I think he fetched the gun, loaded it, and threatened her with it. I think he fired the shots into the floor. I don't know why. Anger maybe? And when the police arrived, he made her take the blame for everything.'

'Apparently the neighbour who called the police has been concerned about Mrs Tennant for some time,' said Joyce.

'Why?'

'The neighbour thinks Mr Tennant is a bully.'

'So it appears the man is quite unpleasant towards his wife,' said Philip. 'I don't think Mrs Tennant is the aggressor in this. I think it's Tennant. He could be our man.'

'You think W Division here have arrested the wrong person?'

'They acted on the information they had when they arrived at the scene,' said Philip. 'But I think you need to get Tennant arrested now and questioned.'

Chapter 59

'IT WILL BE interesting to find out how Joyce gets on with Mr Tennant, won't it?' said Philip the following morning. 'I hope he's the culprit. In fact, he must be. He clearly has a habit of threatening people with revolvers.'

An attractive lady in a lemon-yellow coat and matching cloche hat entered the shop.

'Oh look, it's Mrs Dashwood,' said Augusta.

Mrs Dashwood grinned as soon as she saw Philip. 'I thought I might find you in here! There was no answer at your door.' She was accompanied by a young maid carrying an enormous hamper. 'I've brought a little thank you gift for you. Where shall I put it?'

'That's very kind of you, Mrs Dashwood,' said Philip. 'There was really no need. Here, let me take it from you.' He leant his stick against the counter and the maid handed him the hamper. 'Goodness, that's heavy. I hope you haven't carried it far.'

'Only from the taxi outside,' said Mrs Dashwood.

Philip placed the hamper on the counter. 'How's your husband faring?'

'He's recovering alright. He was only in the hospital for a day in the end. He had breathed in a little of the smoke. He'll be off work for about a week so he can recuperate properly. The cook is making lots of delicious meals for him. Unfortunately, he's become afraid of the dark and will only sleep with the light on.'

'I'm sorry to hear it.'

'I've told him to pay a little more attention when he's travelling on the tube now. Fancy being so engrossed in a newspaper that you don't even notice you've stepped off at the wrong station! I suppose many of us have got off at the wrong stop absentmindedly. But one that's in pitch darkness! Very silly. He certainly won't be making that mistake again. Anyway, Philip, you were of great comfort to me during my ordeal, so there are some treats in the hamper for you by way of a thank you.' She stepped forward, rested a hand on his shoulder, and placed a delicate kiss on his cheek.

This display of affection surprised Augusta. Philip coloured deep red. 'You've displayed more than enough generosity, Mrs Dashwood,' he said. 'I didn't do a great deal to find your husband.'

'But I would never have got through it without your support! I shall be recommending your services to all my friends.'

'Thank you, Mrs Dashwood. That's very kind of you indeed. I suppose it's only polite that I should offer you a cup of tea in my office.'

'Oh, that would be lovely, Philip!'

'Would you like to join us, Augusta?' he asked.

'No, I should get on with some work here. But thank you.'

Philip nodded and went upstairs to his office with Mrs Dashwood and her maid. Augusta felt annoyed Mrs Dashwood had appeared again. She had hoped she wouldn't see her again now her husband had been found.

The hamper remained on the counter. Augusta stepped behind the counter, surreptitiously unbuckled the lid of the hamper, then peered inside. Among the items in there, she spotted a large fruit cake, bottles of port and whiskey, a box of toffees and a box of peppermint cream chocolates. She hoped Philip would share them out over the coming days.

She buckled the hamper again and the pile of *Aristo* magazines caught her eye. She recalled Fred had added some more editions recently. Although she wasn't interested in looking at more photographs of toad-faced James Stevenson and the beautiful Crawford sisters, she didn't want to miss anything.

As she leafed through the pages, she realised what a boring, repetitive life James and his friends led. She caught sight of another photograph of the Crawford sisters looking like shop mannequins. 'Imagine having to decide which glamorous outfit to wear every evening,' she said to Sparky. 'And having to fuss about with hair and all that make-up to make yourself look perfect. It must take hours to get ready. And for what?'

Sparky cocked his head as he listened to her. She felt sure he agreed.

A photograph caught her eye. 'Goodness, this is a surprise.' She peered closer at it. 'Surely that's not... I think it might be.'

She turned and went into the workshop where Fred was tidying the piles of books awaiting repair.

'I need to go out for a short while,' she said. 'Would you mind the shop for me?'

Chapter 60

AUGUSTA RETURNED to the shop after lunch, keen to speak to Philip.

'He left about twenty minutes ago and told me he was going to Scotland Yard,' said Fred.

Augusta sighed. The information she had just discovered couldn't wait. 'Very well, I'll go there now.'

'Is everything alright, Augusta?'

'I'm not sure.' She smiled. 'But thank you.'

'For what?'

'For bringing in those *Aristo* magazines. I need to tell Philip about them.'

'Tell him what?' said Fred. But Augusta was already heading for the door. 'I'll explain later,' she called back over her shoulder.

TEN MINUTES after flagging down a taxi on Great Russell Street, Augusta was at Scotland Yard.

She made her way to Detective Sergeant Joyce's office, only to meet Philip and Joyce coming out of it.

'Augusta!' said Philip. 'This is a surprise! You've just heard?'

'About what?'

'Gunshots have been fired in Pall Mall. Two people have been hit.'

Augusta followed them out of the building. Philip loped as quickly as he could with his walking stick while Joyce dashed on ahead.

'Pall Mall is where Anthony Grimston's office is,' said Philip as they crossed the road to Trafalgar Square. Up ahead, a flurry of pigeons took flight as Joyce jogged through them.

'You think it could be something to do with Grimston?'

'Possibly. Or Stevenson. I don't even know if he's out of hospital yet.'

They passed Nelson's Column and headed for the northwest corner of Trafalgar Square which led to Cock-spur Street and Pall Mall.

'This leg is so frustrating when you need to move quickly,' said Philip. 'I've always lived in hope it will improve but I'm not sure it will.'

The pace was frustrating, but Augusta tried to remain patient. On Pall Mall, they came across Joyce speaking to a group of constables at the junction with Waterloo Place.

'The assailant is believed to be James Stevenson,' Joyce called out to Augusta and Philip. 'He was seen running this way about a minute ago.' He ran off down Waterloo Place.

'You go on ahead with Joyce, you're faster than me,' said Philip.

'Are you sure?'

'Yes! Go. I'll follow you. But be careful!'

Joyce had already reached the tall Duke of York monument at the end of the street. After the monument, a set of stone steps led down to The Mall. Ahead lay St James's Park.

Augusta followed Joyce into the park. She could only assume he had James Stevenson in his sights. Two constables caught up with her.

'We can deal with this,' one of them said as he jogged past. 'No need for you to be involved.'

'I've met him before,' she puffed. 'I can speak to him if need be.'

She tried to keep up with the constables as best she could, but it wasn't easy running in heeled shoes.

The path led to the expansive, gravelled Horse Guards parade ground. Up ahead, Augusta could see the constables had caught up with Joyce and were passing through the archway in the Horse Guards building. On the other side of the building lay Whitehall. For a moment, they were lost from Augusta's view. Once she reached Whitehall, she looked up and down the busy street, desperately searching for the running figures. Then she caught sight of them on the street directly opposite. She dodged the traffic on Whitehall and her legs ached as she followed Joyce and the constables along Horseguards' Avenue. The street led to the Victoria Embankment and the river.

Was that where James Stevenson was heading?

Augusta caught sight of the constables turning right at the end of the road. When she reached the same point, she could see them on the other side of the road by the riverside wall. About a hundred yards ahead of them, a figure was disappearing through a gap in the wall.

It was James Stevenson and he was heading for the river.

The gap presumably led to some steps and a pier. Augusta ran across the road and dashed along the river wall to where Joyce and the constables had followed Stevenson.

As she reached the steps to the jetty, she saw Joyce and the constables stopped on the steps beneath her. A small motorboat was moored by the jetty and James Stevenson was standing in it. One hand was on the steering wheel and the other was pointing a gun at the police officers.

Augusta stood frozen still, barely daring to breathe.

'Stay well away, or I'll shoot!' said Stevenson.

Nobody moved.

Cautiously, he lowered his gun and started the boat's engine. Joyce took some steps towards the jetty, but Stevenson was quick to respond. He pointed the gun at him.

'Stay away!'

Joyce stopped and Stevenson pulled away in the boat. Augusta watched a cloud of blue smoke rise from the engine as he steered out into the river and headed towards Hungerford Bridge.

There was another motorboat moored at the pier. A bearded man stood by it, open-mouthed and staring.

Augusta was the first to move. She dashed down the wooden steps which led to the jetty.

'Let's take his boat!' she said.

'What?' said Joyce. 'I don't think that's a good idea.'

'But we need to catch Stevenson!' She pushed past him and the constables and ran onto the jetty.

'Can we borrow your boat, please?' she asked him.

'No,' he said, scratching his beard. 'I need it to move these.' He pointed at a heap of sacks on the jetty which appeared to be filled with scrap metal.

'But we need to catch that man!' She pointed at Stevenson out on the river. Sunlight danced in the rippled water and made her squint.

'It's quite alright,' said Joyce, who had now joined her. 'The river police can deal with this.' He turned to the bearded man. 'We're sorry to have troubled you, sir.' The man grunted and returned to loading the sacks into his boat.

Augusta gritted her teeth. James Stevenson was making rapid progress away from them. 'James Stevenson has just shot two people, and he's making a getaway!' she said to Joyce. 'We need to catch him!'

'This is a job for the river police,' said Joyce.

'I'll run up to their station at Waterloo Pier,' said one of the constables. 'It will take me five minutes.'

He took off up the steps back to the road.

'He'll be lucky if he gets there in five minutes,' said Augusta. 'It's more likely to be ten minutes. And in that time, James Stevenson could have travelled some distance down the Thames. And who knows what he's planning? He could board another ship in the port, or even out on the estuary, and it could take him to another country. Do you realise he's getting away?'

'The river police have modern boats, they'll soon catch up with him,' said Joyce.

Augusta watched in despair as James Stevenson's boat disappeared beneath Hungerford Bridge.

Chapter 61

AUGUSTA CLIMBED the steps back to the embankment, hoping to catch sight of Philip. To her relief, he was just emerging from Horseguards' Avenue, hobbling along as fast as he could with his stick.

'Over here!' she shouted out to him. He tried to hobble faster. Her heart thudded as she tried to wait patiently. Philip crossed the road and made his way towards her.

'James Stevenson is in a boat and heading east!' she shouted to him as soon as he was within earshot. 'The river police are being summoned, but we need to chase after him now!'

'Is there a boat we can commandeer?' asked Philip as he arrived, out of breath.

'Yes,' said Augusta. 'There's a man loading scrap metal into it. I asked to borrow his boat, and he refused.'

'What's Joyce doing?'

'Nothing.'

They made their way down the steps back to the jetty.

Philip marched up to the bearded man. 'On behalf of

the Metropolitan Police, we need to commandeer your boat,' he said.

'But I need it.'

'And we need to stop a fugitive. Now hop out.'

The man climbed reluctantly out, and Philip clambered in. 'Come on,' he said to Augusta and Joyce. 'Let's not waste any more time.'

Augusta jumped into the boat and gripped the rail on its side to steady herself.

Joyce hesitated.

'Come on, Joyce, jump in!' said Philip.

'I'm afraid I don't like water, sir.'

'Fine.' Philip asked the bearded man how to start the boat and followed his instructions. As the engine roared into life, he shouted out to Joyce. 'Go back to the Yard and get the message out to all the divisions along the river. Who knows where Stevenson is going to end up? We need them alerted in Kent and Essex too.'

Joyce nodded, and Philip steered the boat out into the water.

THE BOAT BOUNCED and juddered on the water and the sacks of scrap metal tumbled over. Augusta clung onto the rail and the damp river breeze whipped at her face and hair.

'This boat is fast!' said Philip with a grin. He steered it around a group of coal barges moored in the middle of the river and headed for Hungerford Bridge.

'Didn't you say you're not a boat person?' asked Augusta.

'I'm not. But I like speed!'

They passed beneath Hungerford Bridge and Augusta

scanned the river for a sign of James Stevenson. She could only hope they hadn't lost him.

At Waterloo Bridge they passed the river police station. Augusta felt sure the constable wouldn't have reached it yet. James steered around a steamboat which was belching out clouds of smoke and steam.

'I think I can see him!' said Augusta, pointing ahead. It wasn't easy to spot the little boat on the busy river, but she felt sure she could see a motorboat speeding away from them.

'Excellent!' said Philip. 'It's a shame this thing won't go any faster, but as long as we keep him in our sights, we should be fine.'

They veered around more river traffic and passed Temple Pier. Up ahead was Blackfriars Bridge and a railway bridge just beyond it.

'Keep a close eye on him, Augusta,' said Philip. 'I need to pay attention to the river traffic. I don't know the rules for navigating the river. But the man we're chasing probably isn't abiding by them either.' He continued straight on, heading for a gap between two pleasure boats. To Augusta's discomfort, the gap was narrowing as they drew closer.

Pieces of bent and broken metal from the sacks were bouncing around their feet now.

'I think we've got plenty of space,' said Philip as he prepared to pass between the two pleasure boats. Passengers on the boat stared at them as they sped past.

The wake from the pleasure boats made the motorboat bounce and lurch even more. Augusta didn't know how Philip was keeping his balance when one of his legs was weaker than the other. They followed the river's bend to the right, heading for Southwark Bridge. They passed the wharves of Queenhithe and the ancient dock, then passed beneath Southwark Bridge and the railway bridge shortly after it. Up ahead, Augusta could see James Stevenson's boat passing beneath London Bridge.

'He must be heading for a bigger boat,' she said.

'You think he planned this?' asked Philip.

'Yes, he must have done. He must have lain in wait for the two men on Pall Mall. I'm guessing one of them is Mr Grimston. And if he laid in wait for them, then I think he planned this getaway.'

'And a good getaway it's proving to be,' said Philip. 'There's no sign of the river police yet. Hopefully, the constable has alerted them and they've radioed to the station at Wapping. We'll be reaching them soon.'

After London Bridge, the familiar sight of Tower Bridge spanned the river. To the left were the towers and walls of the Tower of London. Beyond Tower Bridge, Augusta could see the tall masts of the large sailing ships moored in London's docks. Augusta hoped the chase would end soon, she didn't like the thought of zigzagging around such large vessels.

'Stevenson's just reaching Tower Bridge now,' she said.

'Has he sped up since we caught sight of him? I wish I knew how to make this boat go faster.'

Tower Bridge loomed over them and then they were past it and out in the upper pool of the Thames.

'Stevenson's stopped!' she shouted.

Then she saw the reason why. Two patrol boats from Wapping river police station were heading for him.

'He's coming back this way,' she said. 'And I don't think he knows we're here. He doesn't even realise we've been following him.'

Philip slowed the boat to a stop. 'Excellent, we can wait here for him.'

'You do realise he has a gun?'

'Yes, and two victims have been shot. I can only hope he's used up all his ammunition.'

Stevenson was now heading directly towards them.

'He must be panicking now,' said Philip. 'We need to intercept him.' Philip slowly steered their boat across Stevenson's path.

'But what if he fires at us?'

'Just duck. He won't have many bullets left, I'm sure.'

Augusta felt nauseous.

Stevenson tried to steer around them but Philip moved the boat in front of him again.

'Get out of the way!' shouted Stevenson. Then he realised who he was talking to. He slowed his boat.

'What are you two doing here?'

As Augusta feared, he raised his gun and pointed it at them.

'Surrender yourself, James Stevenson,' said Philip. 'We know you've shot two men in Pall Mall.'

'And murdered Ellen Foster,' added Augusta.

'You're convinced of that, are you?'

'Yes, I am.'

A deafening shot rang out and echoed off the vast walls of the riverside warehouses. Augusta threw herself onto the floor of the boat. 'I knew it!' she said. 'Get down, Philip!'

'Hopefully, he doesn't have any more—'

Another gunshot interrupted him, and he ducked down next to Augusta. 'He's a madman,' he said.

Slowly, he raised his head and peered over the side of the boat.

'Be careful Philip!' said Augusta. An icy shiver of dread ran through her.

'Surrender!' he shouted to James Stevenson. 'You can't get away now!'

'Yes, I can!' came the reply. 'And I will!'

'Philip, get down!' said Augusta.

Another shot rang out. Philip let out a yelp and clutched his shoulder.

'Philip!' Augusta clambered over to him. He lay grimacing and clutching his shoulder.

'It's alright, I think it just grazed me.'

'Grazed you?' Augusta could see blood between his fingers. She didn't want to tell him the wound looked more serious than a graze.

A roar of a boat engine drew close to them and Augusta screwed her eyes shut. James Stevenson had pulled up alongside them to finish them off. She dared not open her eyes and look at him.

'Is everything alright?'

She had heard the voice before. Inspector Tingle from Wapping river police station. She opened her eyes and called out to him. 'No! Mr Fisher has been hit!'

'We'll get you back to shore as quickly as possible. We've arrested the fellow, though. He's been disarmed, and he's no danger to you anymore.'

'You've got him?'

Philip remained lying on the floor of the boat as Augusta slowly raised herself up and looked out.

The inspector was right. Stevenson was standing in his boat with two police officers. His hands were handcuffed behind his back.

Chapter 62

'THIS IS SCOTLAND YARD?' said Polly Hastings that evening as the taxi stopped in front of the gates. The red and cream brickwork glowed warm in the rays of the setting sun.

'Yes, we're here,' said Augusta. 'Will you be alright explaining to everyone what you explained to me?'

Polly nodded. 'I think so.' She cradled her baby son in her arms.

PHILIP STOOD in Detective Sergeant Joyce's office with his arm in a sling. Stevenson's bullet had caused a superficial wound to his shoulder, and he was under instructions to keep his arm as still as possible while it healed.

Joyce sat behind his desk, looking even more pale and tired.

'This is Polly Hastings,' Augusta said to him. 'She's come here to help us.'

Detective Sergeant Joyce offered his chair to Polly, and she sat down, cradling her baby son.

'Polly has always maintained that James Stevenson murdered her sister,' said Augusta. 'And now she's going to explain why.'

'Just a moment,' said Joyce. 'James Stevenson can't be the murderer. The murderer attacked him!'

'But we know he's capable of murder,' said Philip. 'We've learned the two men shot on Pall Mall this afternoon were Anthony Grimston and his younger brother Robert Stevenson. Grimston is dead but the brother survived.'

'Why did James do it?' said Augusta.

'Because he discovered Grimston and Robert were plotting against him,' said Philip. 'They wanted to remove him as head of the family business. He's being held in Wapping station at the moment.'

'I can't believe Grimston is dead,' said Augusta.

'I'm afraid so. The brother is expected to make a full recovery.'

'Goodness,' said Augusta. 'So James Stevenson murdered Ellen Foster and Anthony Grimston and tried to murder his brother, too. I think he also attacked himself.'

'What?' said Joyce.

'I think he attacked himself to remove himself as a suspect.'

'Impossible. Surely no one does such a thing. How could he have attacked himself? He was pulled from the Thames by the river police.'

'Yes,' said Augusta. 'He chose to jump off Waterloo bridge, which is very close to Waterloo Pier where the river police have a station. Perhaps he even waited for one of their patrol boats to be in the vicinity before he flung himself off the bridge. That way, he would have known that he would be pulled out of the water quickly.'

'You think he did it on purpose? That there was no one else involved?'

'Yes. There have been no other witnesses, have there? I realise it was a quiet time of night, but you would have thought that someone else may have been passing over the bridge at the time, perhaps walking or in a vehicle. And yet there isn't a single witness who has come forward to say they saw the attack.'

'Maybe there was just no one else around? And how do you explain the bruising on his face?'

'He could have inflicted that on himself.'

'Ouch.' Philip winced. 'I can't say there are many people brave enough to punch themselves in the face.'

'He was presumably desperate to remove himself as a suspect in the investigation,' said Augusta. 'And he managed it successfully. Once he appeared to have been attacked, he was no longer considered a suspect.'

'So you're saying Stevenson punched himself in the face and threw himself over the bridge, close to a police patrol boat so he could be pulled out of the water quickly?' said Joyce.

'Yes. What other injuries did he suffer in the attack? I admit he didn't look particularly well when we saw him in the hospital the following day. He had taken a plunge into the icy river. That can't have been a pleasant experience and was bound to have some effect on him. But did he suffer any other bruising on the rest of his body? Any fractured or broken bones? Sometimes when someone is brutally beaten like that, perhaps they might sustain a fracture or have some defensive wounds on their hands.'

'Very true, Augusta,' said Philip.

'The description of the attack just seemed too convenient for me,' said Augusta. 'He claimed he hadn't noticed his attacker following him. And he also said the man's voice was familiar. That could have been a convenient invention, perhaps designed to incriminate Mr Grimston and deflect attention from himself? He wanted to show he was a victim. And we all believed him because we had no reason not to for a while.'

'When I consider it now, Augusta, I can see how he might have engineered the attack on himself,' said Philip.

'Ellen Foster was shot,' said Augusta. 'So if Stevenson was attacked by the same assailant, why wasn't he shot too? If it had been so quick and easy to murder Ellen Foster with a gun, then why did the murderer take their time to beat James Stevenson and throw him into the river instead?'

'It's a good suggestion,' said Joyce. 'But we don't have any evidence.'

'We also have no evidence that another person attacked him,' said Augusta. 'No witnesses to the attack and no witnesses who saw the attacker running away afterwards. The police on the river didn't hear or see anything on the bridge. You would have thought that James Stevenson would have called out for help. They would have heard that, wouldn't they?'

'He said it happened too quickly,' said Joyce.

'He did. But I've been attacked before in a similar manner, and I know that the moment you find yourself helpless at the hands of another person, you instinctively cry out for help.'

'So we now suspect James Stevenson,' said Joyce. 'What about Mr and Mrs Tennant? I thought one of them was a suspect?'

'Mrs Tennant had a motive,' said Philip. 'But we don't believe she was involved.'

'Even though she threatened her husband with a gun?'

'Apparently it was the other way round. Her husband

threatened her and she lied to cover up for him. Fortunately, she has been persuaded to tell the truth and Simon Tennant has been arrested.'

'So Mr Tennant didn't murder Miss Foster?' asked Joyce.

'I don't think so. Even though he's clearly an unpleasant man. Let's hear from Mrs Hastings.' Philip turned to her. 'Do you think James Stevenson is a murderer, Mrs Hastings?'

She nodded. 'Yes. I've always said that. But I've also lied to you.'

Chapter 63

POLLY GAVE A SIGH. Augusta was struck by her resemblance to her sister.

'I'm sorry I haven't been truthful with you,' she said. 'I've been too scared to. William and I have managed to live fairly comfortably in our little home. I received some money each month to cover everything and I didn't really want anything to change. But since Ellen's death, everything's changed.' She gave a sigh. 'I met James Stevenson at The 99 Club.'

'You knew him?' said Philip.

Polly nodded. 'I wasn't a regular visitor because I don't have a lot of money to go to the clubs in the West End. But occasionally, a friend and I would go. James approached me one evening. I didn't know who he was, but I thought he was funny and he paid me lots of compliments. Looking back, I realise now he was trying to charm me for his own gain. But at the time, I was flattered to be shown attention by a gentleman. I didn't realise who his family was. In fact, he didn't tell me who they were until our third or fourth meeting. But I suppose that impressed me even more. I thought he was entertaining and quite handsome and then when I found out he was rich too… I was impressed.'

'When was this?' asked Philip.

'About a year and a half ago. But I've grown up a great deal since then. I realise now how foolish and naïve I was. I didn't realise he said the same things to lots of other women, too. For a while, I truly believed I was special to him.'

'So you met regularly after this first meeting in the nightclub?' asked Philip.

'Yes. He asked to meet me at the club again. I told him I had to save up to visit so he said we could meet before-hand and he would pay for my entry and my drinks too. I felt I would be missing out if I turned him down. I really liked him.'

'How long did your relationship last for?'

'Just over a year. But during that time, I sometimes wouldn't see him for a while. He told me he was a business-man, and that he was very busy running his factories. He also told me he had a lot of friends and he liked to go to parties and socialise. He never invited me to any of the parties he went to. We only ever met in the nightclub and then sometimes he would invite me to his apartment. But I never got to know his friends well, he kept me separate from them. I didn't quite understand it at the time, but I think I know now it was because I was a lower-class girl. I wasn't rich like him and his friends. I think he was a little bit embarrassed to be seen with me. I also suspect he kept me separate because he was seeing other women, too. I realise now I wasn't the only one. I regret how I was completely taken in by him. Ellen tried to warn me.'

'What did she say to you about him?' asked Augusta.

'She told me he was taking advantage of me. And I refused to listen. I just assumed she was jealous! We didn't speak to each other for a few months. James had nothing nice to say about Ellen either. He used to joke that I was the fun, attractive sister and that she was the serious, ugly one.' She hung her head. 'I can't believe I laughed along with that. Ellen had always been the older, sensible one, and I had been in her shadow. I wasn't as clever as her and I didn't want to have a profession like she did. I just wanted to find a good husband. I can't believe I thought for a while that James Stevenson would be suitable.'

'Did he suggest at any time that you would get married?' asked Joyce.

She nodded. 'Lots of times. And to think I believed him! I'm convinced now he said the same thing to lots of other women. But he was the first gentleman I had ever become involved with. And then when I realised I was expecting a child... Well that's when he refused to speak to me.'

Chapter 64

'SO YOUR HUSBAND, Mr Hastings, who died,' said Philip. 'Did he ever exist?'

'No,' said Polly Hastings. 'I had got myself into trouble and so I had to lie to salvage my reputation.'

'How did you feel when you discovered you were expecting a child?' asked Augusta.

'Very frightened. Confused and scared. But I knew the problem could be fixed if James agreed to marry me quickly. Then I wouldn't be in complete disgrace. So I was hopeful the pregnancy meant we could be married. And for a brief time, I pictured myself being the wife of a famous businessman from a wealthy family and having a brood of children with him. I can't believe how stupid I was.'

'You weren't to know,' said Augusta. 'You took him at his word and you cared about him.'

'Yes, I did. I thought I loved him. Perhaps I don't really know what love is. I look back and realise I wasn't thinking straight.'

'You said yourself that you've learned a lot over the

past year and a half,' said Augusta. 'It's unfortunate that you learned the hard way, but you are more courageous and wiser for it. And you have a beautiful son.'

'Yes, I really do love William. I feel ashamed he's illegitimate. I wish I could change that. I suppose many people believe the story that I was briefly married and my husband died. That story gives me some respectability, I suppose. But I don't want to lie to my son when he's older. I want to tell him the truth. And it's going to be difficult.'

'Some children are born into difficult circumstances,' said Philip. 'We can see how much you love your son. That's all he needs.'

Polly nodded. 'Yes. I suppose I shall be both mother and father to him. The only saving grace is that James has been paying me a monthly amount. It's enough for us to keep a roof over our head and to keep ourselves fed. He told me the money would be put into my bank account every month, but that I must never speak to him or contact him again. He says he doesn't want my son to know he's his father. So I don't know what I shall say to William when he's old enough to ask about him. I know that once he's at school and he sees other children's fathers, he's going to want to know about his own father.'

'If you want to tell him the truth, then you should,' said Augusta. 'Don't let James Stevenson tell you how you should raise your child.'

'But what if he stops the money? That's been my biggest worry in all of this. That's why I have said nothing about him. I've kept this secret because I need his money for William.'

'His family is very wealthy,' said Philip. 'I'm sure an arrangement can be made for them to support William. How did Ellen feel about the way James treated you?'

'She was angry. I think she was upset when I wouldn't

listen to her and continued to see him. I ignored her warnings, and it frustrated her. I thought she was just being difficult, but I realise now she was being protective. She was doing what any older sister would have done. And then when he deserted me... She was very furious. I told her it was all my fault, that she shouldn't get so upset about it. But it didn't make any difference, she was angry at him. She wasn't angry with me at all. I think she understood how much I regretted what I'd done. She saw him as a man who had taken advantage of me. And it was true. And so she decided to take her revenge. And she did that through her writing.'

'That's why she wrote the articles about his factory?' asked Philip.

'Yes. She had already begun doing some research on him when I was still seeing him. She told me she didn't like him even then. So she had already found out quite a lot, and she knew about the factories that he ran. She had also heard of some accidents at the factory in Deptford, and so she went there and started speaking to some of the workers. I guess that's how she came across Kitty Beaumont.'

'When we spoke to James Stevenson and his adviser, Mr Grimston, both of them claimed the articles didn't bother them too much,' said Philip.

'I know James was upset about them. He came to see me.'

'So you saw him again more recently?'

Polly nodded. 'He called at my home and he told me to speak to Ellen. He said the stories had to stop. He said they were untrue. I told him that Ellen was very committed to her work, and she wouldn't listen to me. I told him to take it up with the newspaper. Maybe he did, I don't know.'

'So did you speak to Ellen to persuade her to stop writing the articles?'

'I didn't persuade her, no. I told her I was worried he would stop sending me money if she continued what she was doing. But she told me she could help me financially if it came to that. I wasn't sure she would be able to, but she was very committed to writing the articles. I know she had more planned. And I believe, as I did when it happened, that he silenced her.' She shook her head and bit her lip. 'I blame myself!'

'You weren't to know he would do something so horrific,' said Augusta.

'No. But all of this is my fault, isn't it? If I had never gone to The 99 Club, I would never have met him. And if I had never met him, then I wouldn't have been fooled by him. If only I had seen him for who he really was. But I didn't. I allowed him into my life, and it upset Ellen. I can understand why she wanted to take revenge on him, but she paid the price with her life. It's my fault.'

'It's not your fault,' said Augusta. 'It's James Stevenson's fault. He clearly thinks he can treat anybody exactly how he likes. He refuses to take any responsibility for the consequences of his actions. He's clearly cruel, cold-hearted, and malicious. He harmed you, and then he harmed your sister even more. You must not blame yourself, Polly. None of this is your fault.'

'Thank you for your kind words, Mrs Peel. Yes, you're right. He's the one who's ultimately to blame. But I know I allowed him to do it, and it's something I still have to live with for the rest of my life.'

'Well, I never,' said Philip. 'This is quite a story.' He turned to Augusta. 'What made you speak to Polly again, Augusta?'

'A photograph in *Aristo* magazine. Fred brought in some more copies the other day and I happened to look through them this morning. That's when I saw a photograph with Polly Hastings in it. She was at a party with James Stevenson. So I visited you this morning, didn't I Polly?'

The young woman nodded. 'I'm glad you did, Mrs Peel. I was so tired of lying and covering things up. I told the police James Stevenson was the murderer because I really wanted him to be arrested. But I was too ashamed to tell anyone about our relationship and our son. I was worried they would mock me and not listen to me.'

Chapter 65

'WELL I NEVER,' said Lady Hereford in Augusta's shop the following day. 'Jonathan Stevenson will be turning in his grave! I suppose the Stevenson business continues though and will be passed to the next son. What's his name again?'

'Robert Stevenson,' said Augusta. 'But he won't have the family advisor Anthony Grimston to assist him.'

'Which is probably a good thing,' said Philip.

'So James Stevenson killed the adviser and tried to kill his own brother,' said Lady Hereford. 'And the poor news reporter, too. How did he attack her like that?'

'He met her at a bus stop one evening when she was about to travel home,' said Philip. 'He persuaded her to have dinner with him so he could tell her everything she wanted to know about his factory. He told Inspector Tingle at Wapping station that they dined at a quiet restaurant in Waterloo.'

'Not the usual place you'd associate with nice restaurants,' said Lady Hereford.

'No. I think he persuaded her it would be better to talk somewhere out of the way. They left the restaurant after dark, and he pulled her into an alleyway and threatened her with a gun. Then he led her past a timber yard near Hungerford Bridge and down to the riverside where he'd moored a boat. He said the noise of the trains travelling over Hungerford Bridge masked the gunshots.'

'Dreadful!' said Lady Hereford. 'I don't want to hear anything more about him now. What an evil man.' She turned to Augusta. 'And in the meantime, my nurse spotted some interesting articles in the *London Weekly Chronicle* about you, Augusta. Surely they can't print such things about you? It can't be allowed!'

Lady Hereford was aware Augusta had worked for British Intelligence during the war.

'I suppose the stories from those times are going to become known before long,' said Augusta. 'And although I don't agree with what the *Weekly Chronicle* printed, I think it's only fair Sarah should be remembered and not forgotten.'

'I've been meaning to ask about her,' said Fred. 'But I wasn't sure if I was allowed to. Who was Sarah?'

'There were four of us working together in Belgium,' said Augusta. 'Me, Philip, Sarah, and Jacques. Sarah was also a British intelligence officer, and Jacques was French. We were pretending to be Belgian workers.'

'That's impressive,' said Fred. 'You were fluent in French?'

'And some German too,' said Augusta. 'It helped us with the Germans because it meant we were useful to them. Jacques was an ambulance driver, moving injured soldiers and prisoners of war around. He helped quite a few prisoners of war escape and get over the enemy lines back home again. Sarah was a nurse. The Germans thought she was a Belgian nurse, they didn't realise she was

British. She worked with Jacques to get the prisoners out. And they were quite successful.'

'They were,' said Philip. 'They helped a good number of them. Perhaps too many.'

'Why too many?' asked Fred.

'Because the Germans grew suspicious. And they began looking closely at the people who worked at the hospital, Jacques and Sarah included.'

'And what was your role in this, Augusta?'

'I was working in a cafe,' said Augusta. 'I was supposed to be a Belgian waitress. I listened in to the German soldiers' conversations and passed messages back to British Intelligence. Philip was a postman.'

Philip nodded. 'Postmen play a useful role when it comes to distributing messages. There was an entire network of us. But Augusta, Sarah, Jacques and I had worked together for a while, so we were quite close.'

'But then it went wrong,' said Augusta. 'We don't know exactly how. I suspect someone became a double agent because the Germans acted quickly. I received a message from British Intelligence that we had to get out of there as quickly as possible. I had to pass on the message to Jacques, Philip, and Sarah. We already had a pre-arranged plan about how we would escape the town. So that same night we tried to make our getaway in a truck.'

'If we had tried the night before, then we would have managed it successfully,' said Philip. 'But we left it a day too late. The Germans were already on high alert. It wasn't long before we were pursued.'

'We knew they would put up a roadblock,' said Augusta. 'The only way to get out of there covertly was on foot.'

'Through the forest,' said Philip. 'So we abandoned the vehicle and walked.'

'You were trying to make your way through the forest in the middle of the night?' asked Fred.

'We were prepared,' said Augusta. 'We had maps, compasses, and torches.'

'But the Germans had dogs,' said Philip. 'They soon picked up our scent. It was not a leisurely walk through the woods at all. We had to move as quickly as possible. We were only three miles from safety. Three of us made it. And one didn't.'

'Sarah?'

Augusta nodded and felt a lump in her throat.

'Philip and I lost Sarah and Jacques so we were in two pairs for a while. Then we all eventually lost each other. It was each man and woman for themselves. Apparently Sarah told Jacques to go on without her. She said it would be safer if they separated and that she was slowing him down. She told him she could climb trees if she needed to. By daybreak, we reached the safety of the British line. Sarah never arrived. And we don't know what happened to her.'

'Obviously, we feared the worst,' said Philip. 'We never heard from her again. And that's the sad end of the story. Jacques tracked Augusta down last year. He wanted to talk about what happened. Augusta and I were wary about speaking to him because no one was supposed to know what we had been doing in Belgium. But he wanted to talk about it, and we could both understand why. He blamed himself for what happened to Sarah. He shouldn't have.'

'We all felt responsible,' said Augusta. 'I will never forget it. I suppose it's quite nice that her story has been told again by Walter Ferguson, even though his motives were malicious. No one will know Sarah's identity because Sarah wasn't her real name. But I don't think it's safe for Philip or me to have our names revealed. Some people take on a curious and sinister interest in these sorts of events. And officially, they are supposed to remain secret.'

'Well I think you were both very brave,' said Lady Hereford. 'And well done for solving another case. Now then, that's enough about you two. How's my Sparky doing? The only reason I came here today was to see him.'

Chapter 66

IT WAS a week later when Augusta received the letter. It was written in a loping, untidy hand:

I was told not to set foot in your shop again, so I thought I'd write. Well done on catching James Stevenson. Now you've established the identity of the killer, you probably regret ever suspecting me.

Don't worry, there are no further articles planned about you for the time being, Mrs Peel.

But I have uncovered something interesting. There never was a Mr Peel, was there? And Augusta is not your real name.

I wonder what secrets you're hiding? I shall keep digging.

Yours faithfully,

Walter Ferguson

The End

Historical Note

Kentish Town is two miles north of central London. South Kentish Town tube station opened as Castle Road in 1907 and was a station on the Charing Cross, Euston and Hampstead Railway line. The line was known as the 'Hampstead Tube', then later integrated into the modern-day Northern Line. Castle Road was renamed South Kentish Town in 1917, but it had low passenger numbers. The station was closed in 1924 (a little detail I chose to overlook when writing a book set in 1921!).

The station reopened as an air raid shelter for Londoners sheltering from bombing during World War II. Most deep level tube stations in London served this purpose at the time. These days, the station building still stands. It has the distinctive red tiles and arched windows of the iconic tube stations built at the beginning of the 20th century. The building has been converted into a shop and - at the time of writing this in 2024 - the station beneath is now an escape room experience.

The story of a man accidentally disembarking at South Kentish Town tube station seems to be an urban legend.

Some sources maintain it happened, whereas others dismiss it as fiction. The incident inspired a poem. Called *The Tale of Mr Brackett,* it was published in the London Underground staff magazine with accompanying illustrations. The unfortunate Mr Brackett accidentally got off at South Kentish Town while engrossed in his newspaper and was stuck in the station for a week before being picked up by a tube driver. The famous poet and writer, Sir John Betjeman, picked up the story and wrote *South Kentish Town* in 1951. It was a short story about Mr Basil Green, an income tax official, who was too busy reading the *Evening Standard* to notice he'd got off at the closed station. There's no resolution to Mr Green's predicament, he appears to be trapped there with the "dreadful silence in the station… and he could imagine huge hairy spiders or reptiles in the dark passages." I imagine John Betjeman was punishing the character for being a tax official!

Whether or not there's truth to the story, it lives on and provides the inspiration for one of the games in the escape room which now occupies the station. It's called *The Lost Passenger.*

Pall Mall is a prestigious street in St James's and runs parallel to The Mall – the road which links Buckingham Palace with Trafalgar Square. Pall Mall was constructed in the 17th century and is known for its exclusive gentleman's clubs such as the Reform Club and the Athenaeum (both of which now admit women members). St James's Palace stands at the eastern end of Pall Mall and serves as one of the many residences of the royal family.

Deptford is a riverside area of London on the south side of the Thames. It was on the popular pilgrimage route from London to Canterbury Cathedral in Kent and gets a mention in Chaucer's *Canterbury Tales* written in the 14th century. In the 16th century, King Henry VIII established the royal dockyard at Deptford which gave the area important maritime significance for a few centuries. Shipbuilding and ship maintenance were dominant industries.

The Elizabethan poet, playwright and rumoured spy, Christopher Marlowe, is buried in an unmarked grave at St Nicholas church in Deptford. He was murdered in a fight at the Deptford home of a widow, Eleanor Bull, at the tender age of twenty-nine. A plaque at the church commemorates him.

London's shipbuilding industry and dockyards waned in the early 20th century, and this led to economic decline in the areas which had relied on the industries. Redevelopment projects in the area have attempted to redress this, and today Deptford is a lively and diverse area of south London.

Pleasure boats on the Thames became popular in the 18th and 19th centuries, and the arrival of steamboats and paddle steamers made day trips on the Thames a popular activity in Victorian and Edwardian times. In the 1920s, day excursions on pleasure boats were still common with people keen to visit destinations such as Kew, Richmond and Hampton. Longer excursions took passengers downstream to resorts on the Kent and Essex coastlines. Although some of these latter locations have declined in popularity, pleasure boats are still a common sight on the Thames. Speedboat tours are also available – perhaps Augusta and Philip's speedboat chase could be recreated!

The Baker Street Murders

An Augusta Peel Mystery Book 7

When Augusta Peel discovers a mysterious message in a book she's repairing, her enquiries take her to Baker Street. But events turn sinister when she learns the address is linked to an unexplained death.

Enlisting the help of Philip Fisher and his detective agency, Augusta attempts to solve a crime which has remained hidden. Can the pair possibly match the skills of Baker Street's most famous resident, Sherlock Holmes?

It's not long before the body count rises. And when someone discovers her true identity, Augusta's own secrets threaten to catch up with her.

Find out more here: mybook.to/baker-street-murders

Thank you

Thank you for reading this Augusta Peel mystery, I really hope you enjoyed it!

Would you like to know when I release new books? Here are some ways to stay updated:

- Like my Facebook page: facebook.com/ emilyorganwriter
- Follow me on Goodreads: goodreads.com/emily_organ
- Follow me on BookBub: bookbub.com/au- thors/emily-organ
- View my other books here: emilyorgan.com

And if you have a moment, I would be very grateful if you would leave a quick review online. Honest reviews of my books help other readers discover them too!

Also by Emily Organ

Penny Green Series:

Limelight
The Rookery
The Maid's Secret
The Inventor
Curse of the Poppy
The Bermondsey Poisoner
An Unwelcome Guest
Death at the Workhouse
The Gang of St Bride's
Murder in Ratcliffe
The Egyptian Mystery
The Camden Spiritualist

Churchill & Pemberley Series:

Tragedy at Piddleton Hotel
Murder in Cold Mud
Puzzle in Poppleford Wood

Also by Emily Organ

Trouble in the Churchyard
Wheels of Peril
The Poisoned Peer
Fiasco at the Jam Factory
Disaster at the Christmas Dinner
Christmas Calamity at the Vicarage (novella)

Writing as Martha Bond

Lottie Sprigg Travels Mystery Series:

Murder in Venice
Murder in Paris
Murder in Cairo
Murder in Monaco
Murder in Vienna

Lottie Sprigg Country House Mystery Series:

Murder in the Library
Murder in the Grotto
Murder in the Maze
Murder in the Bay

Made in the USA
Middletown, DE
05 April 2024

52647655R00158